SOUP
AHOY

ALSO BY ROBERT NEWTON PECK

A Day No Pigs Would Die

A Part of the Sky

Soup

Soup and Me

Soup for President

Soup's Drum

Soup on Wheels

Soup in the Saddle

Soup's Goat

Soup on Ice

SOUP
AHOY

Robert Newton Peck

illustrations by
Charles Robinson

Alfred A. Knopf · New York

THIS IS A BORZOI BOOK
PUBLISHED BY ALFRED A. KNOPF, INC.

Manufactured in the United States of America
2 4 6 8 10 9 7 5 3

Library of Congress Cataloging-in-Publication Data
Peck, Robert Newton.
Soup ahoy / by Robert Newton Peck ; illustrated by Charles
Robinson. p. cm.
Summary: A radio contest, the impending visit of actor Sinker
O. Sailor to their small Vermont town, and rumors of a black
pearl in Wet Lake spur Soup and Rob on to a spectacular
nautical disaster.
ISBN 0-679-84978-5 (trade)
ISBN 0-679-94978-X (lib. bdg.)
[1. Boats and boating—Fiction. 2. Contests—Fiction.
3. Vermont—Fiction. 4. Humorous stories.]
I. Robinson, Charles,   1931– ill. II. Title.
PZ7.P339Soaale 1994 [Fic]—dc20   93-14097

In memory of
BENNY HILL,
a gifted British clown, whose comedy,
generosity, and kindness deserve honor

—R. N. P.

Robert Newton Peck

500 Sweetwater Club Circle
Longwood, Florida 32779

Howdy y'all!

Soup and Rob cannot answer every individual letter. Group letters, sent flat (unfolded) will receive special attention.

Please be sure your package has a <u>school</u> address, not a home address.

Thanks. Thank you for being a fan and a friend.

Your pals — ♡
Soup and Rob.

SOUP
AHOY

1

"Go," said Soup.

He let loose of Ripper.

The race was entirely Soup's idea. He went crazy over any kind of a *contest*. Earlier, he'd said, "Rob, I bet a cat can lap up a bowl of milk faster than you can."

"Like heck," I'd told him. "I can beat a cat with my hands tied behind my back."

So now the race was on!

Two big bowls of milk sat on the floor, awaiting the pair of contestants. Ripper trotted to his bowl a bit quicker than I crawled (on my knees) to mine. Soup had crossed my hands behind me, then knotted them together with the string from his mother's apron.

The rest of the apron was wrapped around my waist. Part of it was dragging.

Bending to the bowl on Soup's kitchen floor, I lapped a first sip. I could see Ripper's tongue lapping away with catlike quickness.

Soup was the umpire.

His given name, however, wasn't Soup. It was Luther Wesley Vinson, and mine was Robert Newton Peck. Uproad, above the town of Learning, Vermont, our farms sat next to each other. Soup was my best pal. And worst enemy.

I tried to suck up a mouthful of milk.

"No slurping," said Soup in his official voice.

"Ripper's slurping," I said, drooling milk from my mouth, and coughing.

"No he isn't." Soup laughed. "However, as you can see, he's already more than a lap ahead of you."

No cat, I then decided, was going to defeat me in a milk-lapping race. Lowering my snout, I began to give the milk a tongue-lashing. But I'd forgotten one important precaution. Balance. It's not easy to kneel on a hard wooden floor and slobber from a bowl with both hands tied behind you. So, lurching forward, my face plunged into the milk just as I inhaled. Milk flooded both my nostrils. And one of my ears. My nose sank.

I sputtered out a wheeze.

"Try drinking it," Soup suggested, "instead of breathing it."

Beside me, Ripper had shifted gears into a higher

4

intake speed. But I wasn't about to allow a *cat* to win. I began to lap with a renewed fury. Without breathing. It felt as though I was fixing to choke, and made me wonder if a kid could drown in a kitchen.

Ripper, I noticed, had stopped.

Eyeing my bowl, then his, Ripper could see where most of the milk now rested. Not in *his* bowl. That was when Ripper decided to visit the dish that contained more milk.

My bowl.

"Hey," I said, "he's drinking *mine*."

Soup shrugged. "Well," he said, "as I see it, there's only one way for you to be a winner, old tiger."

"How?"

"Do what Ripper's doing," said Soup.

That's what I did. Switching bowls, and kneeling in a puddle, I lapped at what little was left of Ripper's milk. I licked up every drop. Raising a drippy face from the bowl, I grinned triumphantly at Soup.

"Rob," he said, "you're the champ."

"Sorry, Ripper," I told my opponent.

I had to admit that Ripper was a gallant loser, seeming not to care. He just finished the milk in my bowl, sat up, licked a paw, and purred.

Soup petted him.

"Rob," said Soup, as he began to unbind my hands, "congratulations, old top. To tell you the straight of it, I certain didn't believe you'd outlap Ripper. You win the prize."

"A prize? What is it?"

Soup grinned. "Another bowl of milk."

I burped. Long and loud, a big basso belch that would have made a tugboat envious.

Mrs. Vinson (Soup's mother) walked into her kitchen to eye us with well-founded suspicion. After taking notice of the two bowls, the cat, my tied-up wrists, her apron, plus the milk all over my face, my shirt, and her floor, Mrs. Vinson slowly placed her hands on her ample hips, and then shook her head.

"I'm not," she sighed, "going to ask."

Remembering my guest-in-someone-else's-house manners, I politely wiped my face, using my sleeve. Then, while Soup finished untying my hands, Mrs. Vinson used her mop handle to point at the kitchen clock.

We looked at the time.

"Yikes," said Soup.

It was already half past four! Panic seized us. Jumping like a pair of spooked rabbits, Soup and I tore out of the kitchen in a mad gallop. We couldn't miss our favorite late-afternoon weekday radio program. Reaching the giant Emerson radio in the Vinsons' parlor, Soup leaped for the dial.

Click!

Breathlessly we waited for it to warm up to static level. It final did. Elbows on the frayed rug, Soup and I were sprawled and ready, itching for fifteen minutes of pre-chore broadcasting bliss.

BVOOOOOOOOOOOOOOT, sounded the customary opening foghorn whistle. Somewhere, beyond an imaginary wharf in Radioland, sea gulls cried, and ocean waves pounded in foaming fakery. Eight bells clanked in pairs.

"It's time," gusted a windblown voice through the salty mist. "Little sailors and sailorettes, prepare to shove off and ship out for another danger-packed adventure of-. . ." He paused.

Morse code piped the three familiar letters:

$$\cdot \ \cdot \ \cdot \ - \ - \ - \ \cdot \ \cdot \ \cdot$$

S.O.S.

"It's time for Sinker O. Sailor."

With breathless anticipation, Soup and I nudged our bellies an inch closer to the enormous radio. Sinker was our hero. A man whose chest bore a secret tattoo.

"I can't wait," I said.

"Brought to you," gushed the announcer, "by Soggymushies, the breakfast food for kids who only want the box tops. Soggymushies taste almost as good as the box they come in. No vitamins. No minerals. Just a blend of sawdust, chemicals, and toxic waste.

"And *now*"—the announcer's voice lowered to a more intimate tone—"we continue our hair-raising voyage. As you recall, Sinker O. Sailor and his crew of ninety-nine shipmates washed overboard in a typhoon, swam through sharks to an uncharted South Sea island, and were about to be captured by man-eating headhunters, all of whom eat like . . . well, like savages. But wait! Sinker suddenly hears a scream."

GBLAAAAACHT.

"Say," said the voice of our hero, Sinker O. Sailor, "could that be a scream?"

The scream came again, and louder.

"Well, now," said Sinker knowingly, "scuttle my porthole, if that wasn't a genuine call for help, just as sure as there's salt in the . . . Somebody spilled coffee on my script. Salt in the . . ."

"Cellar," prompted the announcer.

"But," said Sinker, "at least that tom-tom-tom-tom stopped beating."

BOOM boom boom boom.

BOOM boom boom boom.

BOOM boom boom boom.

"Bail my barnacles," said Sinker, "if that pesky old cannibal drum hasn't started up again, in that fever-ridden and insect-infested jungle."

"Help!" a child's voice cried out.

"Bless my bilge," said Sinker, "if that ain't a little girl calling for help, I'll hoist a rudder or poop a deck. In fact, I'd bet my secret tattoo on it."

A drum pounded.

BOOM boom boom boom.

"Should I rescue that poor unfortunate victim," Sinker wondered aloud, "or should I stay right here where it's safe, up to my neck in quicksand and encircled by poisonous snakes?"

"Rescue her," Soup and I prompted the radio.

Sinker O. Sailor must have heard us, because what followed was the sound of a plumber uplugging a clogged drain.

BLOOOK . . . SHUFFLE . . . SHUFFLE.

"There," he said. "I managed to jump out of that there deep pit of deadly quicksand and hopscotched through the snakes."

"Help! Help me."

"Can I do it?" Sinker asked. "It won't be easy, because it could be *one against a hundred!*"

"Wow," said Soup, "one against a hundred."

"Boys and girls," asked the announcer, "do you suffer from . . . *nutritional overload?* Don't worry. Instead of protein, luckily for you, little shipmates, Soggymushies contain K-21, the amazing new chemical that kills weeds, strips varnish, and poisons rats."

"What about Sinker?" asked Soup.

"And now," the announcer added, "back to our death-defying adventure, into a steamy jungle, with Sinker O. Sailor."

"Here I go," said Sinker, "wading deeper and deeper into a steamy jungle, even if it's going to be one against a hundred."

A bloody battle ensued.

"I hope," said Sinker O. Sailor, "that a deadly blowgun will not be shooting poison darts at me."

"How do they poison a dart?" I asked Soup.

"Easy," my pal answered. "They merely dip the pointed tip into their school cafeteria's food."

"Do I hear a dart blowing my way?" asked Sinker.

HISSSSSSSS . . .

Sinker said, "Thar she blows."

"Golly," I said to Soup, "poor Sinker doesn't stand a chance. Not when the odds are one against a hundred."

BOOM boom boom boom.

"However," said the announcer, "the rescue was a sea breeze for Sinker O. Sailor, even though it was a hundred against one."

The battle was over.

A little girl was rescued.

"Whew," sighed Sinker to his crew. "We won."

Ninety-nine of Sinker's shipmates (plus Sinker) all agreed that this had been *one* of the most savage cannibals they'd ever had to fight.

"Ahoy," said the announcer. "Here's how *you* might get a genuine Sinker O. Sailor white sailing cap . . . absolutely *free!*"

"Free," panted Soup.

"Free," came my echo.

It was the magic word, for us, as well as for every other sucker. The irresistible worm. But there was a hook.

"All you do," said the announcer, "is tear off the top of your mother . . . Sorry, I read the wrong line. All you do is pester your mother to drop whatever she's doing, even if it's tending the baby, and *run* to the grocery store to buy thirty-nine boxes of Soggymushies."

"Why?" asked Soup.

"Here's why," said the announcer. "There's a *contest!* That's right. A contest that *you* can win." We listened, eager to learn more. "Sinker O. Sailor," the announcer told us, "wants to visit your hometown. Why? *To meet you . . .* in person!"

"Wow," said Soup.

Neither of us could believe that maybe we'd be actual shaking hands with our hero.

"Here," said the announcer, "is how you enter the contest. Tear off thirty-nine Soggymushies box tops, along with telling us *why* you'd like to meet Sinker O. Sailor. Mail your entry, and your *cap size,* to:

Sinker O. Sailor
Station WGYP
Rutland, Vermont."

"Rob," said Soup, "let's do it."

"How many box tops have we collected so far?"

"Seven," said Soup. "So all we need to do is corner only thirty-two more."

He was superhuman at subtraction. Otherwise Soup Vinson was subhuman.

"Thirty-two even," said Soup.

"Even," said the announcer, "if you don't win first prize, the ten best entries will receive a *free* consolation prize. An official Sinker O. Sailor white sailing cap," the announcer announced, "absolutely *free.*"

Soup and I looked at each other.

"Free," we whispered in restrained rapture.

Then I saw Soup's smile begin to fade. "Rob," he said soberly, "we won't need thirty-nine box tops."

"We won't?"

"No," said Soup. "We need seventy-eight. Because it'll take that many for *two* sailing caps."

My heart sank.

2

Soup smiled.

"No school today," he said.

Yet here we were, the entire school (all twenty-eight of us), standing in front of our little one-room schoolhouse, in the custody of Miss Kelly.

We were going on a field trip, Miss Kelly had informed us. A hike. Our teacher, however, wasn't coming along. Instead, our leader would be the county nurse, a very large lady named Miss Boland. She was Miss Kelly's best pal.

"Now," said Miss Kelly, "I doubt that our dear friend Miss Boland will arrive here in her usual white nurse's uniform. So be forewarned. She may be in her field trip togs."

"What are field trip togs, Miss Kelly?" I asked.

Miss Kelly sighed. "Having known Miss Boland for so many years, if she appeared in a football suit, or robed as a Hindu snake charmer, I wouldn't be at all surprised."

A car honked!

Turning my head, I saw and heard a familiar car coming our way. Miss Boland's little black Hoover coupe. It was more than a mite amusing, I mused, that one of the largest people in Learning actual rode around in the town's smallest car.

The Hoover wheezed to a halt.

Out of the car exploded someone we weren't at all prepared to see. Oh yes, it was Miss Boland. But to-day, she wore a pith helmet, winged breeches, high-top laced boots, and a backpack. Around her neck hung a pair of black binoculars, a large compass, a camera, plus a little silver whistle. At her waist, a U.S. Army canteen and a Red Cross first-aid kit. This human photo opportunity also carried a long-handled butterfly net.

"I'm ready," announced Miss Boland.

"So," said Miss Kelly, "I see."

"On a field trip," said Miss Boland, "I've always been a believer in being thoroughly outfitted."

"I'm relieved," said Miss Kelly, "that you decided not to bring along your accordion."

Fumbling into a shirt pocket, our nurse produced a small silvery object. A harmonica.

14

Soup winced.

"With any luck," he whispered, "she'll lose it, or get it all clogged with spit. Or asthma."

"Now then," said Miss Kelly to her friend, "please don't get lost and make the whole town worry."

We all remembered the last hike. The Volunteer Emergency Squad was called out to locate our nurse. They spotted her roaming around in the marsh that's not fifty feet behind her house.

Miss Boland held up a hand.

"Panic not," she said. "I brought a map."

"Good," said Miss Kelly. "Have fun."

Miss Boland blew her whistle.

TWEEEET.

"Troops," she said, to all twenty-eight of us, in her authoritative hike-leading voice, "form a line, single file, and prepare to march."

Twenty-seven kids hurried to line up behind Miss Boland. One, however, didn't hustle at all. There was no need for haste. Not for the meanest critter in all captivity.

Janice Riker walked very calmly to the front of the line . . . ahead of Eddy Tacker, our school's toughest boy. Yet no one (not even Eddy) dared to *think* about protesting: "Hey, Janice, you can't buck the line ahead of all of us, because we were here first."

Nobody said boo.

Survival, in Learning, was never confronting or messing with or enraging Janice Riker. She was the

only industrial-strength kid I ever knew. In a fight, her opponent usual requested that Janice use brass knuckles, as they punched you softer than her fists.

"Forward," commanded Miss Boland, *"ho!"*

Soup and I lucked out.

The pair of us were the last two kids in line. It was, however, the best position. Because we both hiked far away from the possible jabs and kicks from Janice Riker.

There wasn't a kid, large or small, in the entire county that didn't avoid Janice, even if such a detour meant having to climb over barbed wire, or cut through a bull pasture.

Her favorite game was *Doctor*.

You might be thinking that playing Doctor with a girl is a lot of fun. Well, it isn't—not when Janice is always the Doctor. And, believe me, you sure do have to be Patient until she final cuts you loose.

"Looks like," Doctor Janice had said one time, "we may have to amputate. Now where did I leave my chain saw?"

As we all hiked along, I could spot her, up ahead, following our nurse. She was built a lot like a small Miss Boland, only shorter, and stockier than a county fair blue-ribbon steer. Janice didn't look like a kid. More like a tractor.

Our field trip was mostly uphill, and so some kid asked Miss Boland where we were heading.

"It's a surprise," Miss Boland answered with a wink.

It took about a hundred hours, but we final arrived, stopped, and hauled in a breather.

"Here we are, troops," puffed Miss Boland.

"Where are we?" Soup asked.

Miss Boland smiled. "Wet Lake."

Our nurse explained the name. Wet Lake existed up here on Lonesome Mountain because it was fed by melting snow and several cold springs beneath its surface.

"It is called Wet Lake," said Miss Boland, "because such icy water always seems wetter than warm water."

In Vermont, there isn't any warm water.

It's all piped in from the North Pole. And very cold. On a sunny day in May, such as today, lakes and ponds can often still contain frozen bits of winter. By summer, the ice is all melted, but the water is still liquid ice.

However, by Labor Day, a few of the hardy hazard a swim. A brief one. In about a minute, your teeth chatter, your muscles all cramp, and your skin turns color.

Blue.

"Troops," said Miss Boland, "let's chow."

Janice claimed that she once started a fire by rubbing two Boy Scouts together, but Miss Boland said that we'd do it the Indian way. With matches.

We had all brought hot dogs. These we roasted on sticks until they were totally black or fell into the fire. Our marshmallows met a similar demise. For a beverage, we helped ourselves to a sip (one sip) of Wet Lake. One sip was plenty. The water was burning cold.

Yet it was a beautiful scene.

A light clear sky, inky blue water, and a few May flowers here and there along the shore. Fragrances of pine and balsam inhaled with every breath. We chewed little wintergreen leaves, hard and crisp, but full of free flavor. It almost made me forget about Sinker O. Sailor and the radio contest.

"This is the life," said Miss Boland.

Soup asked her about Wet Lake.

"Well," said our nurse, pointing to the south, "the icy waters of Wet Lake flow in *that* direction, over there. The water forks at an island. One branch drifts lazily the long way. The other branch, however, is very dangerous water. It rushes down Suicide Flume."

"Interesting," said Soup.

"Now," announced our nurse, "it's entertainment time."

Seated on a bed of brown pine needles, her spine braced against a tree trunk, Miss Boland tooted out her only selection, *Beautiful Dreamer,* on the harmonica. It couldn't have been called music. Our nurse's harmonica didn't deserve being called a musical instrument. Instead, it was closer to some sort of a vacuum cleaner. Soup and I gritted our teeth until *Beautiful Dreamer* scraped and squawked to its merciful awakening.

"Out there." Miss Boland pointed to the center of little Wet Lake. "That's where it is. So they say."

"What's out there?" Soup asked.

Miss Boland's face turned serious. "Deep in those mysterious waters of Wet Lake," she told us, "lies . . . its *treasure!* In a sense, buried treasure, away down in the depths."

"What sort of a treasure is it?" I asked.

"It all happened years ago," said Miss Boland. "A circus had come to town. Their oldest elephant got loose. Some say that the elephant climbed up here to Wet Lake to die." Her voice became a spooky whisper. "Other folks claim that the elephant is still here. They sometimes come to scout for tracks."

I looked around. "Up *here,* Miss Boland?" I asked her.

She nodded. "But there's more to the story. At the time, a man was rowing a boat out on the lake. Rumor holds that the elephant tipped over his boat."

"Did he drown?" Soup asked.

Miss Boland shook her head.

"No, he saved himself. Clung to his boat and drifted to shore. Yet his prize possession fell overboard. Sank to the bottom. It was his *treasure,* so he claimed. And the local legend goes . . . it's still there." She pointed. "Out there in Wet Lake."

"Was it gold?" asked Soup.

"Silver?" I asked.

Miss Boland shrugged her shoulders.

20

"My guess is neither one. Because," she said, "the fellow who lost his treasure wasn't rich. Not in the least. But he disappeared shortly thereafter. Perhaps *death* sealed his lips forever. All we know in Learning is this. He called his lost treasure by a very strange name."

We held our breath, speechlessly, waiting for our county nurse to give us a hint about the sunken secret. At last she spoke. In a whisper.

"He called it . . . Black Pearl."

3

The news spread in Learning.

Soup and I were walking along Main Street, listening to everyone gabbing away about the radio contest, and the possibility of meeting, in person, a famous celebrity

Sinker O. Sailor.

Some people heard him on the radio. Others didn't. Yet not a soul in town could seem to talk about anyone else. Not much went on here in Learning. A radio contest was considered a major event.

A few people, I presumed not many, even went so far as to trek a special trip to Graziano's Grocery to purchase a box of Soggymushies. Neither eaten nor opened, they were saved as souvenirs. Box tops and all.

Turning a corner, Soup and I met a familiar and welcome face. It was our county nurse and field tripper.

"Hi, Miss Boland," we chirped.

Miss Boland was entirely in white, looking cleaner than a Sunday shirt. She gave us a big smile.

"Howdy do, boys. Keeping out of mischief?"

"Yes'm," we lied.

"No doubt," said Miss Boland, "you young rascals have already heard the news, about Mr. Sinker O. Sailor's contest."

"We heard it on the radio," Soup said.

"Me too." Miss Boland winked. "Sometimes, if'n I'm to home early enough on a weekday afternoon, I confess I'll sometime tune in WGYP and listen to one of Sinker's seagoing adventures on the radio. And I've wondered about his secret tattoo."

"We want to mail in our entry," I said.

Miss Boland nodded. "Good." Her face suddenly turned sober. "I certain hope you tell Station WGYP your correct cap size, in case your letter makes the best ten."

"We sure will," said Soup.

"Small," I added.

"Yes," said Miss Boland, "I'd estimate for sure and certain that *small* is the size you'll need." She patted our heads.

Soup asked, "When do you figure Mr. Sinker O. Sailor will arrive here in town, if somebody here wins?"

Miss Boland shrugged her shoulders. "Oh, I haven't any idea. Some people say it'll be right away soon."

"Gee," said Soup, "I hope so."

"Me too," I said.

Miss Boland looked around in several directions, then spoke. "I've spent my entire life here in Learning. A nice town. But it'll be rather exciting to meet a world traveler like Sinker, a sea captain who's been to exotic places, and sailed a clipper ship over those choppy oceans."

"It sure will," I said.

Miss Boland grinned. "I'm glad, providing there's a local winner, that the town's going to do something special in his honor."

My mouth fell open in surprise.

"We *are?*" I asked her.

Miss Boland's hand shot up quickly to cover her mouth. "Oops," she said. "I s'pose I just let the cat out of the bag." She stooped down to whisper to Soup and me. "Now don't breathe a word of it, because nothing's final just yet. It's supposed to be a *secret.*"

"Okay," we whispered.

"As you know, boys, I serve on the Town Council. I'm the only woman on it. The only lady crazy enough to bicker with those nine old skinflints who haven't spent a penny since the Crusades. But I just came from a meeting. And I nagged them into it."

24

"Into what?" Soup asked her.

"Promise not to tell?"

We promised.

"Well, then, here's the deal. My plan is to hold a big special Sinker Day, with an outdoor picnic. Maybe it'll make old Sinker realize that he's still popular." Her face drained its smile. "I know somebody who works at WGYP, and she says that the radio station manager wants to cancel Sinker's show."

"What's the trouble?" asked Soup.

"Well," said Miss Boland, "there's a story going around that WGYP thinks that Sinker's getting *too old*. Aren't we all? So maybe somebody ought to hatch up a scheme to keep Sinker O. Sailor from sinking. Throw him a big festival."

"Honest?" I asked.

She nodded. "But," warned Miss Boland, "nobody on the Town Council could consent on a place for the party."

"And," said Soup, "*you* had an idea."

"You betcha," said Miss Boland. "Can either of you two lads ever recall a time when I didn't opinionate?"

"No," we agreed.

"So," said Miss Boland, still whispering, "I told them that the only place to hold a fitting reception for a sea captain would be by *water*."

"On a lake?" Soup asked.

"Well, perhaps not *on* a lake, but neighborly close enough to water to create a nautical scene for the celebration. That was when old Mr. Prinklehouse announced that his south cow pasture had a puddle and it would be the ideal site, so he'd be willing to rent it to the town for a very reasonable fee."

"What happened?" I asked her.

"Needless to say," said Miss Boland, "each one of those old coots had a hunk of property to rent out. Nobody consented to a thing."

"Until you spoke up," said Soup.

Miss Boland giggled. "Right," she said. "So I suggested *town land* instead of a private plot for profit. They all grumbled, but at least they all compromised."

"Where?" I asked.

Miss Boland said, "The Thumb."

"That's near water, all right," said Soup.

"It sure is," I agreed. "It's that thumb of dry land where the crick makes a horseshoe bend."

"Just below the flume," said Miss Boland.

The Thumb was almost an island. Actual, it was a peninsula, like Florida, and the same shape. The crick flowed along on three sides.

"That'll be watery enough," said Miss Boland. "And the roar of the rapids will supply us with a proper background sound, as if we're all at sea."

"Perfect," said Soup, "for a radio show."

"And it'll be a real picnic?" I asked.

"For sure," said our nurse, raising her right hand as though swearing an oath.

"Hot dogs?" asked Soup.

"For a nickel," said Miss Boland. "Just enough to cover expenses. Root beer'll be a nickel too. I don't yet know about ice cream, or cotton candy. Depends on the weather report."

"Maybe," said Soup, "the town of Learning ought to give Mr. Sinker O. Sailor some sort of a present. You know, to give his spirits a boost." His eyes narrowed. "Or perhaps another kind of surprise."

Miss Boland snapped her fingers.

"Good idea, Luther," she said, using Soup's formal name instead of Soup. She called me Robert a lot.

"What'll we give him?" I asked.

Miss Boland scowled in thought. "Beats me," she said softly. "What in the dickens would a sea captain want, other than a rocking chair, or a footstool?"

"A boat?" I asked.

"No."

"A canoe?" Soup suggested.

"Nope," vetoed our nurse. "Nothing watery. But, on second thought, a proper gift might be some sort of a doodad that a naval person would find fitting. Let's all think."

We thought.

The three of us paced to and fro.

"I got it!" said Miss Boland, with a crisp snap of her fingers. "Why didn't I think of that football game before. Of course. It's so obvious."

"A football game?" Soup inquired.

"In May?" I also asked.

Miss Boland made a face. "No, not a football game. What I meant to say was, not just *any* old football game. I mean . . . the big Army-Navy Game."

Soup and I looked at each other. Football is an autumn activity. Did our county nurse need a *head* mechanic?

"Last fall," Miss Boland explained, "my cousin Alfred actual took the train to somewhere near Philadelphia, or nearby, and he attended the Army-Navy football game. He saw the whole thing. In person."

"So?" we asked.

"So *this*. Each team paraded out an animal mascot. The Army Cadets had a mule. A real live mule. The Navy—I think they're called Biddies—had a mascot too. But it wasn't a mule."

"What was it?" I asked.

"The perfect gift for a sailor," said Miss Boland. "They claim that every old seagoing salt dreams of a farm. And, by golly, have we ever put our fingers on the right present to give our celebrity . . . that is, if he comes."

Soup and I held our collective breath.

Miss Boland laughed, and then she told us what she had in mind to present Mr. Sinker O. Sailor, on Sinker Day.

4

"This is it," said Soup.

"Our very last house," I said.

Soup knocked at the dark oaken door.

We waited. Hearing footsteps from within, I knew that Soup and I were in luck. Somebody would be coming to the door.

Somebody came.

"Whattayawant?" he snapped with a scowl.

It was old Mr. Jubert. He was a senior citizen known for disliking children, especially those that could muster up enough gumption to knock at Mr. Amos Jubert's front door.

"Rob," said Soup, "you handle it."

Mr. Jubert frowned down at me.

"Well?" he growled.

I cleared my catchy throat. "Uh . . . Mr. Jubert . . . we only need seventy-one more. All we have is seven."

"What say?" He leaned closer.

"Uh . . . sir, Soup and I are trying to collect seventy-eight of 'em. But we need them to send away."

"What in blazes are you talking about?"

"Box tops," said Soup.

"I don't have any boxes," Mr. Jubert spat. He cupped a hand to his ear. "What in thunder is this all about?"

"A free cap," I said.

"Are you some sort of a nut?"

"No," I said. "Honest, Mr. Jubert, we have to collect seventy-eight box tops of Soggymushies."

"Soggywhatties?"

"Soggymushies. It's a cereal."

Mr. Jubert's sour face darkened. "I don't like cereal," he snorted. "And, furthermore, I never like anyone who eats it. Man or beast."

"Oh," I said.

"What's the name of that infernal tripe again?"

"Soggymushies," said Soup.

"Right," I said.

"And you two young hellions expect me to feed you breakfast cereal, here at my house, for *free*."

"No," I said. "We don't want the *cereal*. Honest. Soup and I don't eat it. Nobody does."

"In fact," Soup broke in, "we dislike cereal so much

that we don't like anybody who eats it . . . except for Sinker O. Sailor. He's our hero. He even wears a secret tattoo on his chest."

"Z'at so?" Mr. Jubert asked.

We nodded.

I'd often wondered about Sinker's tattoo. Did he really have one? If so, what was it? For certain, it would be something to do with ships at sea.

"Sinker O. Sailor," grumbled old Mr. Jubert. "He's on the radio. Don't like him. And I'm glad that WGYP might be yanking his show off the air."

But then, before Soup or I could comment, Mr. Jubert opened his door an inch wider.

"Soggymushies, eh?"

"Yes, sir," we both said, trembling.

"That's quite a coincidence," Mr. Jubert told us. "Well, don't just stand there like idiots. Come inside."

We entered by cautious inches. His house smelled sort of musty and dusty, a bit like old Mr. Amos Jubert himself.

"Buttinski eats 'em," he cackled.

Soup and I looked quickly at one another, then turned to face Mr. Jubert again.

"Buttinski?" Soup inquired.

"That's right. He's my goat. And I don't get along with *him* either. Come on back to the kitchen." We followed Mr. Jubert. "That tomfool goat of mine won't eat anything else, except Soggymushies. Tried 'em once myself. Dreadful stuff. Tastes like a helping of dead bedbugs. They're only fit to feed to visiting relatives."

Mr. Jubert opened a kitchen cabinet.

"Nope," he said. "Wrong shelf." Closing the cabinet door, he opened another. A larger one. Double doors.

I couldn't believe what I saw. Blinking, I began mentally to count the boxes of Soggymushies. There must have been over a hundred.

"Got 'em on sale," said Mr. Jubert.

"Holy cow," said Soup Vinson.

"I don't believe it," I said.

"Like I said," Mr. Jubert continued, "that blasted goat of mine eats a box of that pap every day. Sometimes more. I keep hoping it'll do him in. Because I don't want my goat to outlive me."

"What do you do with the box tops, Mr. Jubert?" I asked the old gentleman.

"Save 'em. I got 'em stored around here somewheres. Thought they might come in handy. People say you can send 'em away and get prizes." He squinted down at us. "For *free*."

I nodded.

Soup nudged me.

"Mr. Jubert," said Soup, "if you happen to have enough Soggymushies box tops, we could send away for *three* caps. One for you, one for Rob here, and one for me."

"I don't want a cap," he said. "I never liked caps,

nor did I ever trust anyone who wore one." Mr. Jubert peered at us over the half-moon lenses of his spectacles. "I s'pose," he told us, "you expect me to give you all my box tops for *nothing*."

"No," said Soup. "We'll work for them. Rob and I will do a chore for you."

"We will?" I asked Soup.

"Yes," said Soup. "That's only fair."

"All right," said Mr. Jubert, rubbing his hands with a sly smile. "The chore is to come over every day and feed my goat."

Soup asked, "Where is he?"

"Out back." Opening his kitchen door, Mr. Jubert pointed to a square pen in his backyard. "There's old Buttinski."

I blinked.

So did Soup.

I'd expected to see a small goat, or at least one of middle size. Buttinski could have pulled a freight wagon. Up a hill.

"Is he friendly?" Soup asked.

"Not to me," said Mr. Jubert. "Nobody's ever been friendlike to me in seventy years." He kicked the door. "Can't figure out why."

Buttinski looked our way and frowned. Then he sort of growled as if his stomach was upset. He pawed the dirt and snorted. It sounded like swearing. Buttinski reminded me of Janice Riker.

"Well," asked Mr. Jubert, "we got a deal?"

Buttinski's feedbox wasn't near the fence. It was in the exact center of the pen. This presented a prickly problem. To nourish Buttinski would require opening his gate, entering the pen, dumping the Soggymushies into the feeder box, then escaping while still alive, but wounded.

"We'll do it," said Soup.

Mr. Jubert raised his eyebrows.

"You will?"

Soup nodded. "But," he said, "we sort of have to have our box tops today, sir. Please."

"How come?"

"To send away," Soup said.

"That's right, sir," I added. "If'n we don't send in our seventy-eight box tops by tomorrow, we can't enter the contest."

"How many do you need?" he asked us.

"Seventy-one," I answered.

"That's a lot of box tops to boys who haven't yet done me a lick of work."

"We promise," said Soup. "Don't we, Rob?"

I smelled trouble. At the moment, I could also smell Mr. Amos Jubert's goat. The smells were a lot alike.

"Okay," I agreed. "I promise too."

"Done," said Mr. Jubert.

He spat on his hand, shook hands with Soup and then with me. The old geezer had the grip of a crab that was running for office.

For some strange reason, Mr. Jubert seemed eager

to close the deal. Very eager. It made me wonder why. Why? It was possible, even probable, that Soup Vinson and Rob Peck were stumbling blindly into a trap. And the snare might be a square pen with an ornery goat.

Mr. Jubert was already tearing the box tops off his vast supply of Soggymushies. To my amazement, Soup was even helping him.

"There," said Mr. Jubert at last, counting the box tops for the fourth or fifth time, just to make certain that Soup and I had not been overpaid. "Seventy-one even."

"Thanks a lot, Mr. Jubert," I told him, extending my hands for his box tops.

"Not so fast," he said. "You boys agree to feed Buttinski until every last flake of that confounded cereal is used up?"

Soup raised his right hand.

"Sir, we promise. Don't we, Rob?"

Reluctantly I nodded. "We promise."

"Okay, here's your box tops. Do you two rascals know where to send 'em?" Mr. Jubert squinted at the back of the cereal box. "Says here to state your *cap size*. Small, medium, or large."

"What size do you think we wear?" I asked.

"For you two pinheads," said Mr. Jubert, *"small."*

He banged the door closed.

That evening, Soup and I tied all seventy-eight of

our Soggymushies box tops into a tidy bundle. Then we addressed and stamped a very large envelope:

Sinker O. Sailor
Station WGYP
Rutland, Vermont

"All those chores were easy," said Soup.

"Right," I sighed. "Because now we have to sit down and compose the most important letter of our entire lives."

Soup nodded. "Rob, as I see it, there's only one way we can win the radio contest."

"How?"

Soup grinned. "All the other kids will write letters that *want* something for themselves . . . like a free sailing cap, or, better yet, to shake hands with Sinker O. Sailor."

"So do we."

Soup agreed. "True, but it might be nicer if we tell Sinker what a couple of polite farm kids would like to *give him*. To cheer him up. Golly, I bet Sinker's feeling mighty low, worrying that the radio station might discontinue his show."

I thought about it. Soup's ideas rarely made sense, yet this one held water. Besides, giving a present to Sinker O. Sailor was okay, as he'd given even Soup and me plenty of hours of radio thrills. For free.

"Rob, do you agree?"

I agreed.

Pacing the floor of his bedroom, to and fro, Soup Vinson dictated while I wrote it all down, changing a few of Soup's phrases into my own.

Dear Mr. Sinker:

Thanks for being our hero.
You're also a friend.
Please come to our town.
We aren't rich people. But we'll share our home-grown food with you, with lots of fresh milk from our Holstein cows.
Everyone will smile.
You can actually do a radio show here. We'll help. Best of all, we have a gift for you that you'll always remember. We can't buy it in a store.
Instead, we'll make it ourselves. It won't be fancy. It'll only be like us... yours forever,

Luther Wesley Vinson
Robert Newton Peck

5

"Samoa," said Miss Kelly.

Soup and I were in school, side by side.

Our teacher stood before us, pointer in hand, its tip now resting on some little island on our wall map of the Pacific Ocean. Most of the map was blue.

Before me, on my desk, lay my open textbook. It was entitled *Frontiers of Geography*. But, at the moment I wasn't paying too much attention to whatever Miss Kelly was saying about the pretty white gardenias of Samoa. Instead, I was being attentive to the one flower of my life. The blossom of my bliss.

Norma Jean Bissell.

In my personal and private opinion, Norma Jean was (and would forever be) the sweetest girl in the entire universe. Well, at least in all of Vermont. I'd not visited many places.

There she sat. Like a gob of honey.

A mere three seats away. Only a matter of feet, yet too distant for my liking. As opposed to sharing a bench with Luther Wesley Vinson, I longed to be seated next to Norma Jean Bissell.

If only for a day.

In the past, during my few unguarded moments of romantic daring, I had presented Norma Jean with a gift or two that I deemed adequate enough to cement our coupling. A particular offering, that I'd been convinced would gladden her heart, was the tail of a gray squirrel. Most of the fleas removed.

As a topper, I also gave her a slightly rusted tomato can that contained several of my best night crawlers. These were earthworms, at least five inches long, perfect in baiting a hook for catching catfish, or crappies.

To my amazement, Norma Jean Bissell's reaction to these spiritual sacrifices had been less responsive than my expectations.

She'd only said one word:

"Yuk."

Our token exchanges, I had to admit, hadn't been a one-way street. Norma Jean, on my birthday last winter (February 17), had sneaked me a surprise that, to say the least, left me more than a mite mystified.

She'd wrapped it. And—you won't believe this—

even added a blue ribbon, the color of a summer sky. It looked too pretty to open.

Yet open it I did, with eager and fumbling fingers, all of which were more than slightly soiled.

It was *soap!*

I had looked at her in near disgust.

"Rob," she'd said softly, "you're the nicest boy I know. But you'd become a whole lot nicer if you washed. For *me?*"

"Wash?" I'd asked, cringing at such a repugnant idea.

Norma Jean nodded. "Try it."

"But," I had tried to explain to her, "I'm a *boy.*"

A year or so earlier, I'd mastered the unique difference between boys and girls. Girls, I'd concluded, all smelled a lot like Miss Kelly. Boys, on the other hand, smelled either like worms or like the mud they lived in.

This particular fragrance, I learned, wasn't at all what Norma Jean Bissell had planned for Robert Newton Peck.

Soup elbowed me.

"Rob," he hissed, "you're doing it again."

"Doing what?"

"You're gawking at Norma Jean."

"No I'm not."

"Are."

"Ain't."

"Are."

"Luther and Robert," warned Miss Kelly.

That was all she said.

For some reason, perhaps known only to her, our teacher said "Luther and Robert" about a dozen times a day. Allow me to explain that she said it *with her back to us,* and how she managed to monitor our conversation was more than either Soup Vinson or I could fathom.

"Fathom," said Miss Kelly.

I faked attention.

"A fathom," Miss Kelly went on to say, "is a water measurement, and it constitutes a depth of six feet."

I yawned.

"Over in Samoa," our teacher was now explaining, "a South Pacific diver sometimes dives to a depth of several fathoms, holding his breath, to collect a netful of oysters."

I stole a glance at Norma Jean.

Soup jabbed me.

"Oysters from the ocean," said Miss Kelly, "supply the island inhabitants with food, such as a delicious oyster stew. But every once in a while, an oyster will produce a special bonus. Can anyone guess what that is?"

Norma Jean Bissell lofted her elegant hand.

"I might know, Miss Kelly," she said in a voice that could have accompanied the harp of an angel.

Miss Kelly nodded at Norma Jean.

"A pearl."

Beside me, Soup suddenly stiffened.

"That's correct," said Miss Kelly. "A pearl."

Looking to my right, I noticed the face of Luther Wesley Vinson. Mischief, I suspected, was muddling in his mind. I began to wonder exactly what Soup was pondering.

I prayed it wasn't some crazy *plan*.

"No," I hissed, "I won't be part of it."

"Not even," Soup whispered back, "if it just might impress the living heck out of a girl whose initials are N.J.B.?"

"Wrong," I said. "Count me out."

"Pearls," said Miss Kelly, "as Norma Jean said, do come from the ocean oysters. Most of them are white. However, every once in a while, the divers bring up a pearl that isn't white."

"What color is it?" asked Soup.

"Black," said Miss Kelly. "And black pearls are even more valuable than the white ones."

"Ah," said Soup. "It all fits."

"No," I told him. "No tricks."

Yet my brain was remembering what our nurse, Miss Boland, had told all of us during our field trip up to Wet Lake. Somewhere, out beneath those deep and cold mountain waters, lay a special Black Pearl.

My spine shuddered.

Not because of the cold Wet Lake water. It was due to the fact that I suspected Soup Vinson had begun to devise one of his daring disasters. A prank that would plunge me, Rob Peck, into capers beyond my coping.

"*No,*" I repeated.

It didn't do any good. The familiar look on Soup's demented and demonic face was, at this moment, expressing it all.

"The Black Pearl," he whispered to me, "just might ignite Norma Jean Bissell a bit more than a slimy night crawler."

I had to admit it.

Soup was right. All I had gleaned so far, from my secret longings for Norma Jean, was a bar of soap. Its label read Extra-Strength.

"And so," said Miss Kelly, still persisting in assuming that we were enrapt with the dietary habits of the pearl divers of Samoa, "we learn that, in many a tropical culture, the citizens have discovered how to harvest a treasure from the sea."

"Treasure," said Soup.

Now, I feared, there was no stopping him.

Luther Wesley Vinson had clenched the proverbial bit in his teeth, and his brain had shifted gears. To full sail.

"Please," I begged him. "No plan."

"It can't miss," he mumbled. "Rob, this particular idea is, to borrow a phrase, a sure bet."

A *bet,* I knew, was a gamble.

Right then, my hands started to sweat. From this moment on, I vowed, I'd have to be totally on guard, or else I'd be entangled in some senseless insanity . . . involving . . . *what?* An oyster? Samoa? My pearly teeth chattered in panic.

"Cheer up, Rob," whispered Soup. "It isn't going to be as bad as you're imagining." He chuckled. "Not some shallow venture. This one will have depth."

I couldn't even watch Norma Jean Bissell.

"No," I begged.

"You can't be serious, Rob."

"Yes," I said. "I mean *no.*"

"Honest?"

I nodded. "My mother told me that whatever your next escapade was, I'm to take no part in it. Papa's also warned me. We are *not* to get into trouble. If so, there's no going to the picnic."

Soup smiled. "Now that's funny."

"What is?"

"*My* mother told me the same. You see, I have my parental fossils convinced that all of our troublesome trials have always been *your* ideas. Not mine."

"You rotten rat," I said to Soup.

"Is that any way to address a best pal?"

"Soup," I said, "I'm not just a pal. I am sort of trying, believe it or not, to *survive.* To get through childhood in one piece. Without going to jail or the cemetery."

"Don't panic," Soup told me.

"I am not a panicker."

"Neither am I," said Soup. "But don't forget, right

after school is over, you and I have a chore to do. You haven't considered going back on your promise, have you?"

"Not me," I told him.

"Good," said Soup. "Because in about an hour, you and I have to face up to our appointed task."

I knew what Soup meant.

Buttinski.

6

"Let's take a detour," said Soup.

It was after school. The two of us, so I thought, were on our way to the backyard of Mr. Amos Jubert.

Soup, however, had another route in mind.

"This isn't the way to Mr. Jubert's," I said.

"Rob, old top, we'll get there. But first, let's sort of swing by for a brief visit at our very favorite place. Our haven of havoc and hope."

I knew where.

The Dump.

Soup Vinson's family wasn't wealthy. Neither were the Pecks. Between the two of us, there was rarely a penny to spare or spend. Stores, to supply our needs, were totally beyond our budget. In the past, The Dump had usual presented Soup and me with a vast array of trash and treasure, all of it available for the taking. No charge.

Soup's pace quickened.

"Ah," said Soup, "here we are."

There I stood, in wonder, as Luther Wesley Vinson went blissfully bounding into the many mounds of mystery. To him, a trip to The Dump was a visit to a free candy counter.

For me, however, it signaled a warning.

A red flag!

Without pause, Soup began his search with wild-eyed enthusiasm. The expression on his face could only be described as a look of intense intent. His eyes blazed with bunko.

I climbed a mountain of mess.

"What," I asked Soup, "are we after?"

"This is it!" he yelped, tugging and yanking on what appeared to be a long green snake. He final jerked it loose, then held it up for me to appreciate.

"A garden hose?"

"It's a start," said Soup. "And," he added, "here's a little flag of *Samoa!* I recognize it, Rob. It was in our geography book."

"What else do we want?"

"Find a rope," Soup said, "while I locate a gasoline can, and a see-through plastic tray or a cookie sheet. We need one transparent, like glass."

I found rope.

"And we'll need a tire pump, one that works, and a pair of army boots," said Soup.

Soup was removing a long black-rubber inner tube from a very large truck tire.

"We won't be able to pump up *that*," I told him. "There's a hole in it big enough to throw a rat through."

Soup sighed.

"Rob," he asked, "don't you get it yet?"

"No."

"Then search around for some wire. A few old coat hangers will do the trick." His face cracked a wide smile. "Aha!" he exclaimed. "Here's a nifty little item I never thought of."

He waved it triumphantly in the smelly air.

"What is it?" I asked.

"A dog harness," Soup announced.

"We don't have a dog that small."

"It's not for a dog," Soup said, tossing me the harness. "Here, put our prizes in a pile."

He disappeared to the yonder side of another trove of trash, while I busied myself in a quest for wire. *Bang! Clang! Bonk!* Soup was beating on something or other. And it sounded weirdly metallic.

"Rob!" he hollered. "I found it."

"Found what?"

"A gasoline can."

The can was shaped like an elongated cube, higher than wide. Four flat sides and with a handle on top. It was bright red.

50

"For gasoline?" I asked Soup.

"We'll need gas," he told me, "where *we're* going. But, you see, the gas is our assorted atmosphere."

I froze.

"I'm not going," I said.

"Nonsense," said Soup. "This'll be the hour of heroes. To establish our fame, far and wide."

"I don't want to be famous."

"What *do* you want to be?" Soup asked me.

"Alive," I said.

Ignoring my ridiculous urge for survival, my pal continued his pawing through another assortment of discarded debris. "Rob," he said a bit sternly, "you won't find a pair of boots just standing there. Busy up."

Halfheartedly I looked. To my disappointment, I found a pair, showing them to good old Luther.

"Perfect," he said. "Try 'em on."

They were too large. My feet are about the same as my cap size. Small.

"Hello," said Soup, seeming to have made another lucky uncovery. "Where there's one," he said, "there's gotta be another. Maybe even four or six."

"Four or six what?" I asked him.

For a response, Soup showed me a round black object. It was a flat disk of about a foot in diameter. The thing looked to be heavy.

"It's a stove griddle," said Soup. "Just what you'll need. And the good news, Rob, is that there's *two*."

"A pair of stove griddles. Great," I said, "because

I'd dread having to labor through life with only one griddle."

It *hit* me.

Soup had said . . . *you'll need.*

Somewhere, deep down in the pit of my stomach, imaginary bowls of Soggymushies began to stir, as though alive. I knew the feeling. A sensation of familiar foreboding, and it always acted up when I suspected that Luther Wesley Vinson had given birth to a brainstorm.

"Whatever it is, Soup, forget it."

"Rob, old sport, be not of faint heart." From his lofty perch atop a trash heap, Soup leaped into the air, landing deftly on a discarded bedspring, only to jump even higher.

Again and again.

Boing!

"A garage door!" he shouted. "Find one."

There was no stopping Soup now. It would be folly, I knew, even to try. Already he had launched himself, and me, into some mysterious madness that would march us into mayhem. Soup was a daredevil of destruction, a demon of disaster. I, no doubt, would play a part in his plan.

It was a shuddering sensation.

"An elephant," Soup was singing. "We're going to invent an elephant, old top. An elephant that's *not there.*"

Boing. Boing. Boing.

There he was, before me, bouncing up and down

on rusty bedsprings, singing some idiocy about a garage door. Soon we'd be collecting more garbage, stuff from The Dump that nobody wanted, then assembling it into a lump of lunacy.

Some crazy elephant.

I moaned. Soup, I was deciding, was *not all there*.

Life with Luther was so rarely rest or repose. With my pal, it was a continuous fire drill, and all the warning gongs were clanging.

"Kegs!" shouted Soup Vinson, still bouncing.

I stared blankly.

Boinging slowly to a stop, Soup said, "Rob, I figure four kegs ought to do it."

"Do what?"

"Rob, old sport, the kegs aren't for *us*. They'll go on the four corners of the garage door. It's so obvious."

There I stood, wearing a pair of army boots that were seventeen times the size of my feet, and pondering how I could cut and run. To save myself from whatever it was Soup Vinson was now concocting.

"They're too big," I said, as my bare feet wiggled inside the big boots.

"The kegs?"

"No," I said, "these old boots."

"No problem," Soup told me. "All you have to do, Rob, is wear your sneakers, or another pair of old shoes, and then put the boots on last. And these boots will serve two purposes."

"That's all I have to do?"

"Well," said Soup with a sly wink, "not quite all."

"What am I going to be?"

"A hero. You'll be the star of the show."

"I don't want to do it."

Soup blinked at me in disbelief. "You mean you'd forgo an opportunity to water the eyes of Norma Jean Bissell?"

I gulped.

A mere mention of Norma Jean always prompted the same reaction. I was riveted in reverence. But then, I quickly remembered, the hallowed name of Norma Jean Bissell had always been employed, by Soup, as a wanton worm on a hidden hook.

Rob Peck was the fish. A sucker.

"Okay," I said. "I want to know what we're building."

Soup nodded. "That's the spirit."

"So tell me. Is it really an *elephant?*"

"Rob," said Soup, "we're doing something for Sinker O. Sailor. And, in the process, we are building your reputation, my lad. One that even the friendly folks in Samoa will revere."

"Samoa?"

The Dump didn't look anything like the flowery South Pacific island in the photograph I'd so briefly scanned in *Frontiers of Geography*.

"An average mind," said Soup, "could never conceive the obvious connection between a stove and an elephant."

With my average mind in disarray, I merely shrugged.

"Samoa," repeated Soup. "And if fortune smiles our way, Rob Peck might be able to give his girlfriend a gift of all gifts."

"A garage door?"

Soup shook his head. "A present far more impressive, one that any lucky lady can adore. She'll love the gift and the giver."

Holding my breath, I waited.

Soup told me.

"A pearl."

7

"He's hungry," said Soup Vinson.

There we stood, the two of us, in the secluded backyard of Mr. Amos Jubert. Yet we weren't looking at Mr. Jubert. He wasn't there. All we saw was a very large and powerful billy goat, one with the belligerent name of Buttinski.

"He looks tame to me," Soup fibbed.

"Not to me," I said.

Buttinski, in my personal opinion, appeared to be a direct descendant of *Tyrannosaurus Rex*. But lacking *Rex*'s sensitivity. The goat was now eyeing Soup and me with multiplying mistrust.

"Goats," I said, "can sudden take a dislike to certain people. Leastwise, that's what I've heard tell."

"Not to *us*," said Soup.

I looked at my pal. "Why not?"

Resting his chin on the sawed-off circular top of a fencepost, Soup studied Buttinski.

"Well," he said, "it's all logical. A goat is an animal. Right? And both you and I live on farms. We farmers are kind to animals. We're not cruel. So old Buttinski, no doubt, will understand that what we're bringing him is a meal, instead of mischief."

It sounded reasonable.

Yet the feeder box was in the center of the square goat pen. Not close to the fence. One of us, either Soup Vinson or Rob Peck, would have to carry the Soggymushies *inside* the pen, dump them in the feeder, and then escape without being attacked by a large menacing monster.

One with horns.

During the school year, Miss Kelly had lectured us a lesson in beast behavior. Animals, according to our teacher, were territorial. Usually, she'd stated, an animal minded its own business . . . *until* its turf was invaded. The closer a bird is to its nest, the tougher it will battle.

Buttinski wasn't just near his nest.

He was *in* it.

Soup or I had to be the intruder.

"Maybe," I said to Soup, "our promising to tend old Buttinski wasn't such a savvy idea."

Soup disagreed. "Rob, it was the only game in

town," he insisted. "Our only option. We had to promise Mr. Jubert that we'd feed Buttinski, or we wouldn't have had enough box tops to enter the Sinker O. Sailor contest."

Turning my head, I glanced over to Mr. Jubert's back-door stoop. There it sat, just waiting for us. A box of Soggymushies. Topless. Mr. Jubert had, no doubt, prepared for Soup and me to arrive and perform our promised chore.

"No problem," said Soup Vinson.

"How are we going to do it, Soup?"

"Easy. First off, I'll handle the hairy job. Your part, Rob, ought to be a lead-pipe cinch."

"Really?"

"For sure. *I'm* playing the difficult role in our little charade. Because old Buttinski, if he reckons to get ornery, will be directing his hostility right at *me*. Not at you, old buddy."

Whenever my pal called me *old buddy,* I had learned to suspect that I was about to be set up. Rob Peck, a born victim.

"What do I do, Soup?"

"The easy part. But you don't do anything until I give you . . . *the signal*."

"What's the signal?"

Reaching into a back pocket, Soup pulled out a bandanna. It was a very bright color of red.

"A billy goat," Soup told me, "has a strong inherent dislike for anything that's *red*."

"I thought that was bulls."

"Sort of. But it's a well-known fact that a billy goat hates red even worse than bulls do."

"So?"

"So this, Rob. *You're* to remain outside of the pen, while I try my best to tackle our chief responsibility."

"To feed Buttinski?" I asked.

"Wrong," he said. "My assignment is to create a diversion. Here—I'll demonstrate exactly what I'm talking about."

All I knew about diversion was that it was the opposite of multiplication. Before I could ask, Soup Vinson demonstrated.

Waving his red bandanna, Soup started dancing around the outside of the square pen, hooting and hollering a few choice insults as to Buttinski's lack of intelligence. The goat, I saw, constantly faced Soup as he moved along outside each of the pen's four sides. Several times. Buttinski didn't seem to be in a good mood.

Soup returned to where I was waiting.

"See?" he asked, somewhat out of breath.

"Okay, but what do *I* do?"

"Almost," said Soup, "nothing at all."

"Nothing?"

"Oh, I suppose," said Soup, "we ought to dream up a trivial task for you to handle. Just to keep you from being gored. Excuse me, I meant to say *bored*."

He looked over at the Soggymushies.

"Hey," I said, with a rush of resentment, "you mean to say that you're expecting *me* to—"

"Hold it, Rob. Don't get yourself worked up into a panic. My plan calls for cool heads, two fast-moving feet, and weasel cunning."

Looking at Soup, it wasn't difficult to figure out who the weasel was.

"I want to know right now, Soup. What's *my job* going to be? Is it what I'm afraid it is?"

Soup closed his eyes. "Not at all," he said. "I'm handling the dangerous part. Buttinski will be watching *me*, not you. Because *I'm* the threat to his territory. Me and my noise and my red bandanna."

"Honest?"

"Yes," said Soup. "He likes you."

"He likes me?"

"Right," said Soup. "I'm the one Buttinski hates."

"But he seems to be staring at *me*, Soup, not at you."

"Goats," said Soup, "can turn cross-eyed when they reach maturity. Especially in May."

"Why in May?"

"Because," Soup explained to me in a tired tone, "May is a goat's mating season. That's when they can become a mite cross. I mean cross-eyed."

I wondered if this was true. Luther Wesley Vinson and Truth had never been close comrades. Before I could object further, Soup strolled casually to the stoop, picked up the open box of Soggymushies, and returned.

"Here," he said.

Like a simpleton, I took the box.

"Ready?" he asked.

"No!"

"That's right, Rob. Because I haven't yet given you the *signal*. The signal is . . . when I shake my bandanna up and down. Three times. And holler our secret code."

"Our code?"

"Yes, it'll be our password. Buttinski won't begin to understand it. It's in *code*."

"What's our password?" I asked.

"S.O.S."

"That's a distress signal. Everybody knows that."

"Everyone," said Soup, "except a goat."

"I don't like it," I said, already in distress.

"Rob, be thankful that old Buttinski's only a billy goat, and not a bull elephant. Don't worry."

Rarely am I a worrier. Not until I hear Luther Wesley Vinson telling me not to be one. After that, if there was a country named Worrydom, I'd be king.

"Here I go," said Soup.

He went.

I watched him waving a red bandanna above his head in crazy circles, like a lasso, and shouting at the goat. He ran around the pen two and a half times.

Then, on the far side of the square, Soup stopped. Up and down his bandanna fluttered. Three times. It was certain the *signal*.

Gripping the cereal box with sweating fingers, I waited for the password. It came. In secret code.

"S.O.S.," yelled Soup. "Or, if you really want us to get clever . . . Serve Our Soggymushies."

Buttinski's back was to me.

So I opened the gate, then closed it, dashed in, ran in a full let-out gallop to the feeder box, and poured in every inedible flake of Soggymushies.

"I did it, Soup," I said.

It was a fatal mistake.

Buttinski turned in a split second. I saw him. And worse, *he saw me*. Living on a farm, I'd already learned that whenever you feed an animal, it makes the critter happy. I'd not, however, fed even one of our cows a Soggymushie. I loved our cows too much.

Buttinski snorted, hoofed the ground, and charged. A lot like a bull elephant.

"Run!" hollered Soup. "You're wearing a *red shirt!*"

I ran.

Buttinski followed me.

Around and around and around the feeder box I sped, in terror, with an angry goat closing at my heels. I ran circles until my breath was about to quit. But my legs sure didn't.

"Faster," said Soup, "he's gaining."

I ran faster.

62

How could I have been so stupid as to enter a goat pen while wearing a shirt of bright red?

"Open the gate," I yelled to Soup.

He opened it, and left in a hot hurry.

Out I ran, to safety. We both ran faster than either of us had ever run, faster than when we'd been pursued by Janice Riker. At least old Janice didn't have horns. Buttinski did.

How we did it I'll never know.

But we outran a goat. Maybe because he was older than we were. When we stopped, there was no sign of him. For several minutes, neither Soup nor I spoke. Then my pal had something to say. As I heard him saying it, I realized the trouble we were in.

We had let Buttinski (the cereal killer) *out!*

8

Soup pointed.

It was the next day, after school. Soup and I were in town, in quest of the item that we still needed to collect.

A garage door.

Why we wanted one I didn't know. Yet there we were, poking through an alley behind a row of stores and other establishments on Main Street. Nobody, I hoped, could see us lurking here in the shadows. No one else was in sight.

I looked where Soup was pointing.

"Rob," he said, "we found it."

Searching, I couldn't see a garage door. Or even a garage. But, for some reason, Soup Vinson had instantly ignited into excited. As always, Soup's enthusiasm knew neither bonds nor boundaries.

"There," he said. "It's a wow!"

As we stood at the rear door of a local fraternal organization, The Knights of Saint Bingo, there seemed to be no garage in the vicinity. And, as far as I could detect, no garage door.

Unable to contain his enthusiasm, Soup ripped into a run, leaping into the air, arms wildly flailing.

"Rob, it's a dream come true."

Following, I saw nothing except a very large tabletop. It wasn't the shape of any garage door that I'd ever seen. Garage doors were usual a rectangle. This particular flat object was *round*. But very large. Ten feet in diameter.

"So," said Soup. "The Knights of Saint Bingo recently have obtained a new poker table."

"How can you tell?" I asked him.

"It's obvious," he told me. "Here's their old one. Right here. They've pitched it out. Ready for the scrap heap. Rob, it's ours for the taking. A giant poker chip."

"I don't want it. Soup, you and I have never been dealt even one hand of poker in our entire lives."

Seeing as I was still a kid, I'd made no plans to become a poker player so soon after my weaning.

Mentally I reviewed a comment that my Aunt Carrie had offered, for my betterment, on the sinful subject of gambling. "A deck of cards," Aunt Carrie had warned me, "is nothing more than the Devil's Bible."

Thinking about one particular playing card that Soup and I had found, and secretly kept in hiding, made me sweat. It was a ten of clubs. Guilt prevented my sleeping for a week.

"Soup," I said, "we're *not* gambling."

Eyebrows raised, Soup stared at me in feigned shock. "Of course not," he said. "We don't want to gamble. All we need is this poker table. Lucky for us there are no legs on it."

How we managed to roll a large wooden tabletop so far, and so fast, I will never know. Nor, at the time, did I know why.

I asked Soup. No answer. This I understood, because his brain had already shifted gears. One of his culpable capers had taken root, and sprouted, soon to flower into some blooming butchery that would topple the two of us into a ton of trouble.

"Soup," I said, after we had final heaved and hauled our enormous wooden moon uphill for at least a hundred miles, "where are we going with this tabletop, and *why?*"

"Robert, old top," he grunted, "press onward to our reward. You'll see. For the moment, trust me."

Yesterday, behind the house of Mr. Amos Jubert, I had, in a moment of relaxed vigilance, *trusted* a certain Luther Wesley Vinson. To my detriment. Yet here I was, rolling some idiotic poker table to an unknown location, for no intelligent reason under the sun.

"Why?" I repeated.

"Because," said Soup, "a garage door is square. Or worse, rectangular. This tabletop is round, Rob. We don't have to tote it. It rolls, even going uphill."

"What are we going to put together, Soup?" I stopped. "Darn it. I want to know, and I want to know right *now*."

Soup stopped too.

"You win," he told me.

"So tell me."

"It's to stand on," he said. "Our deck."

"Our *what*?"

"We can't go sailing without something to sail on." Soup paused. "Well, *can* we?"

"No," I said weakly. "We can't."

"Good," said Soup. "I'm so happy you agree."

"*Agree*? I haven't agreed to a single thing. In fact, come to think of it, I haven't willingly gone along with *one* of your insane plans."

I had, but with regret.

"Quite so," said Soup Vinson. "But if any fellow, in this entire world, ever could request an understanding friend, I'd pick you for a pal, Rob Peck. You, and only you, old buddy."

"Why *me*?"

This, I mused, was a question I'd asked of myself time and time again. Why did I have to grow up having Luther Wesley Vinson for a next-farm neighbor? *Why me*?

"Rob," said Soup, as we continued to push, "every

Sherlock Holmes has a Watson. And you, my loyal and noble sir, happen to be mine."

"Am I?"

"Indeed. So keep pushing."

We pushed.

Soup cheered us both on.

"Rob," he chortled, in that weird voice of his that always manifested itself whenever the pair of us were poised toward the compounding of a problem, "only a mile or two more."

Inch by inch, and foot after foot, yard upon yard we rolled our poker-table top. Just when I was fixing to scream, "I quit," Soup Vinson stopped.

"We have arrived," he warbled.

How he could sound so happy after the load we'd lugged, all uphill, was a mystery to me.

I looked around.

We stood at Wet Lake.

Both of us let loose of the tabletop. Over it plopped, appearing to feel as exhausted as we felt.

"Now," said Soup, "the hard part of our trial is mercifully over. Because, instead of four kegs for a square door, all we need for this is . . . something bigger."

He smiled his boyish smile, breathing in the fresh mountain air. Not to mention oxygen and ozone. I had to admit that the atmosphere here at Wet Lake was more than pleasant. But soon, however, Soup

Vinson would be fouling our fortunes with some madcap and mindless misery.

"All that stuff that you and I collected at The Dump," I said to Soup. "Do you have any purpose nestled among our gear?"

Soup grinned.

"Positively," he said. "We'll make tracks to fame. More than that. We'll make *elephant tracks*."

"What?"

"We," he told me, pointing out to the middle of Wet Lake, "are about to launch far more than a boat. We shall, dear pal, propel ourselves up the gangplank of golden glory and establish the names of Robert Newton Peck and Luther Wesley Vinson in the laurel lists of nifty navigation. Ahoy!"

"But all that stuff at The Dump. Is that rotten old junk going to be our cargo?" I asked.

Soup smirked. "Well, sort of."

"Out with it."

"Rob, to be truthful, old sport, our diamonds of The Dump will assemble into something for *you*, not for me."

"For me?"

Soup clapped a hand on my shoulder. "Stout lad, you shall become a legend in Learning. You'll be that one daring boy to confront adventure, face-to-face, and to elevate a mystery into the magic of a miracle. In a way, we are preparing you to meet—if our letter wins the contest—a fellow whose job we are fixing to save. Mr. Sinker O. Sailor."

"Do I meet him on a poker table?"

Soup nodded. "One," he said, "that will be flying our little flag." He grinned at me. "Rob, in only hours," Soup said, gesturing at our gigantic wooden poker chip, "what you witness here and now shall be transformed, almost as if by a magician's wand, into a nautical name of renown."

"What name is our boat going to have?"

Soup beamed. *"Star Of Samoa."*

9

Soup was screaming.

It was the next day, and I'd already seen the R.F.D. mail truck come up our dirt road.

The truck stopped at Soup's house.

Soup had run to meet it. As had I. That's when we discovered that a package had arrived. It wasn't large. Yet the return address on the plain brown envelope said it all:

> Sinker O. Sailor
> Station WGYP
> Rutland, Vermont

Our dreams were about to become a reality.
Twenty anxious fingers began to fumble with the

flap of the package. We final undid it open. And there they both lay, neatly folded, made of genuine paperette.

Two sailor caps.

Size small.

White.

Soup tried on his and I tried on mine. They were identical, and perfect, flimsy reproductions of the very cap worn by Mr. Sinker O. Sailor, hero of the six (or seven) seas. He of tattoo fame.

"How do I look?" Soup asked me.

"Great! How about me?"

"Elephant," said Soup. "I meant to say *elegant*. I can't wait until the kids at school see us under our caps."

"Boy," I said, "will they all be jealous."

Soup said, "They'll turn as green as a hornet."

Also in the package was a *personal letter*, to Soup and to me, typed and signed by none other than Sinker O. Sailor himself:

S.O.S.

Dear Luther and Robert:

Congratulations!
Your letter has been personally
chosen by me and my shipmates at Station
WGYP as one of the ten finalists.
You're still in the contest. You
could win!
Wear your caps with pride. The same
way I always wear my secret tattoo.
In a day or two, you will be informed,
by radio, if you've been selected as the
Big Winner. If so, I'll be shipping out,
heading for your hometown.
So, before I set sail over the
yardarm, or whatever it's called, enjoy
a heaping bowl of Soggymushies. And
heave ho.

Your pal and shipmate,
Sinker O. Sailor

· · · — — — · · ·

While reading and rereading Sinker's letter, I had to brush away a tear. So did Soup. Because it wasn't emotionally easy to receive so moving a message from a hero. A brave old sea captain whose ship might be sunk by WGYP management. Would he lose his show?

Why would the radio station people say that Sinker was *too old*? Heroes, to me, could be all ages.

"Rob, we're lucky," Soup said. "You and I will be maybe meeting Mr. Sinker O. Sailor in person."

"Yeah," I said, "right here in Learning."

Wearing our new white sailor caps (size small), Soup and I looked around town to see if we could locate Buttinski.

No luck.

To apologize for our stupidity in allowing the goat to escape, we worked up the bravery to knock on Mr. Amos Jubert's front door.

He opened it.

"Oh," he snorted, "it's you two. Well, no need to feed my goat today, fellers. Dang animal got loose and run off. Haven't seen hide nor hair. And I don't care. Buttinski and I never got to be close friends. Distant enemies would be more like it. So, if you happen to see my goat, tell him to keep going. And butt out."

Mr. Jubert slammed the door.

Soup and I looked at each other.

"Whew!" said Soup. "We're out of trouble."

I shook my head. "Not, really, Soup. Because it was

our fault that Buttinski got loose and escaped. By rights, we ought to find him if we can."

Soup agreed.

At school, we showed Miss Kelly our letter, and everyone noticed our white sailing caps. I felt especially prouder than pie when Norma Jean asked me if she could wear mine. Or, at least, try it on. Before I got it soiled.

Yet not everyone was happy for us.

Janice Riker and Eddy Tacker, the two tough nuts of the class, seemed to be eyeing our sailor caps with far less than fervent appreciation. I felt a lump in my throat. A big one, when I noticed Janice whispering in Eddy's ear, then staring at me.

And at Soup.

Eddy and Janice (by taking Soggymushies box tops away from a lot of the other kids) had also entered the radio contest. But, as their sour faces now hinted, they hadn't been selected as finalists. Janice Riker and Eddy Tacker had no chance to win.

Soup and I did.

Sure enough, as soon as school was over, and we had all said "Good night, Miss Kelly" to our teacher, Janice Riker and Eddy Tacker were lurking outside.

Waiting to do us dirt.

"Run," said Soup.

He ran. So did I.

We both ran for our very lives. In fact, Soup and I

ran a little bit too fast, considering our situation. Never before, not once in my entire life, did I ever consider that my foot speed might become excessive during an escape from Janice Riker. This particular thought had never crossed my mind.

Yet it happened!

Soup and I, our feet almost flying, had reached top speed. I could feel the wind in my face as I ran. And right then, bad luck, in a double dose.

I never knew that something this awful could happen to me. Yet it did. And, at the same split second, it also happened to Soup.

Our white caps blew off.

Right then, my hand automatically reached up to grab my departing headwear. Too late! All I touched was my own hair.

To my left, out of the corner of my eye, I saw Soup Vinson doing the same thing. Grabbing his bare head. We both stopped. Looking back, I saw our genuine paperette caps floating in the air for a moment. A couple of white birds.

That wasn't all I saw.

Beneath our caps, Eddy Tacker and Janice Riker had also screeched to a stop. There they stood, at anchor, waiting for Soup's cap and mine, with outstretched arms. Fingers eagerly opened.

Our caps floated downward.

"I got one," Janice said.

"And I got the other one," said Eddy.

After sticking their tongues out at Soup and me, Janice and Eddy put our caps on their heads.

"Hey," said Soup, "that's *my* cap."

"Yeah," I said, "and that other one's *mine*."

If you think for even an instant that Janice or Eddy intended to return our sailing caps to us, you've never met those two scabs.

"They're *ours* now," Janice snarled.

"Losers weepers," said Eddy.

"Give 'em back," I heard Soup say. "Please."

Yet I could tell by the quiver in Soup's voice that he never expected our prize caps to be returned to their rightful owners.

Nor did I.

Both of us just stood there, feeling helpless, but afraid to grab our private property. It wasn't fair. One time, when I'd said, "It's not fair," to my father, referring to what I deemed as extra chores, Papa had told me, "Boy, it ain't a fair world."

That was all he said.

During our trip uproad to home, Soup and I hardly said a word to each other. We usual chatted up a blue streak. Not today. The uphill road seemed to be steeper, with more pebbles. And dustier.

Soup kicked a stone.

So did I.

Losing my cap to Janice felt bad enough. But something else inside me felt even worse, because I'd lacked the courage to take back what was mine. For one minute, I'd sure enjoy being an elephant. Big and strong.

I had a hunch Soup might be feeling likewise, even though he was a year and four months older than I.

Then something rather odd happened.

Soup looked at me and said, "Rob, old top, you and I are wasting our time and talents when we harbor a grudge against Janice Riker and Eddy Tacker."

"How so?" I asked him.

"Well," said Soup, "it's sort of like leaving a closet light on when the door is shut. Hatred, as I see it, is a waste of useful energy."

I sighed. "Maybe you're right."

"At my age," Soup said, "I'm not certain about too much. But I feel I'm right about hating. And I'm not going to fritter away a single hostile thought."

"You're not?"

"Nope," he said.

"Rob, as I see it, those two culprits only got our caps. You and I, however, possess something that Janice and Eddy will never have."

I knew what Soup meant, even before he threw an arm across my shoulder (not very gently) and spoke it out.

"Rob," he said, "we got *us.*"

10

Soup came running.

"Hey!" he was hollering at me as I stood just outside our kitchen door.

I looked. He was holding a strange article in each hand. They appeared alike. Soup waved one and then the other.

"I got 'em, Rob."

He sure did have them. I'd seen things like this before, and I knew exactly how they could be used. To pour a lot of liquid into a small hole. Yet I couldn't think of their name.

"Funnels," said Soup. While I was wondering why Soup thought *funnels* were so exciting, he told me. "There are big funnels on every ship! Rob, our equipment is now complete. Let's head up to Wet Lake."

"Now?"

Soup nodded.

We were off, and in a hurry, with Soup setting a very anxious pace. On the way, we stopped briefly at The Dump. Instead of kegs or barrels, Soup selected two long silvery hot-water tanks. Both were bigger than we were. Luckily, they were aluminum, and light.

At least at The Dump they weren't heavy.

But as I dragged them uphill, to Wet Lake (while Soup carried the two funnels), the water tanks began to weigh a ton each.

"Rob," said Soup, "remember when we were really little, how much fun we had *under a table?*"

"I do recall."

"Well," he said, "today's just another day under a table."

"It is?"

"Yup. Because *fun* isn't what you send box tops for," Soup said. "Real fun is what we make ourselves."

"What are we going to do?"

"It's a surprise."

We moved along. Soup was singing a happy song, whistling; even his feet seemed to be skipping into a joyous dance.

"Say," asked Soup, "have you heard the latest?"

"No," I grunted, still lugging both of the tanks.

"Miss Boland," said Soup, "has located a *goat.*"

I stopped.

"Buttinski?"

Soup shook his head. "No, not Buttinski. The goat Miss Boland has obtained isn't a billy goat. It's a nanny."

"A female goat."

"Right," said Soup, "and her name is Nannette. Rumor has it that Nannette is the prettiest goat in town. So I guess Learning is now prepared for a gift to give Sinker O. Sailor." He smirked. "But a goat can't begin to compare to *our* present for Sinker."

I was afraid to ask.

We arrived at Wet Lake.

Tired from tank tugging, I flopped myself down to lean against a tree, to rest. Soup, on the other hand, seemed to be busting out with energy. Yesterday, we had lugged more of our equipment from The Dump up here to Wet Lake. There it lay, right where we'd piled it, hidden behind some juniper bushes.

"Okay," said Soup, "it's time to assemble the gems of our genius."

"What are we going to do first?" I asked.

"Practice walking. Put on your army boots over your sneakers."

While I laced them into place, Soup pulled a pair of tin snippers from his pocket. They looked like a thick pair of shears. He cut four ribbons from the black inner tube. Using these as bulky rubber bands,

Soup secured the two black stove griddles to the bottoms of my boots.

"Walk," he said.

I tried, and did it.

Not easily, as the griddles and big boots made walking a bit labored. As I walked, the griddles left large round imprints along the edge of the lake.

"Keep walking," said Soup. "You're doing great."

While I practiced, Soup used a hose and a tire pump. He pumped air, a lot of it, into both our hot-water tanks.

With the snippers, Soup cut almost an entire side off the red gasoline can, then slid a clear plastic tray in its place, taping it closed and tight. Inside the can he punched a hole, into which he inserted one of the funnel necks. On the outside, he fitted one end of an old twenty-foot garden hose. The other funnel spout squeezed into the hose's far end.

He also attached a second hose to the gas can. Its loose end, however, now led to the tire pump.

I watched in amazement.

"Don't just stand there," said Soup. "Tie our two tanks to the beams on the underside of the poker table. The beams have holes where the legs used to be. Use wire or tape. One tank on one side, one on the other. Parallel. About six feet apart. Or seven. If the ends of the tanks show, it won't matter. We'll sacrifice beauty for stability."

I did it, silently wondering about Soup's stability.

"Now," said Soup, "we're almost ready."

Before I could object, Soup fitted the dog harness to my chest and buckled it, smiling at its perfect fit.

"Am I going to be a *dog?*" I asked.

"No. But it begins with *D*."

I was too timid to inquire.

"In a way," Soup said, "you're going to be an elephant. Let's roll the poker table over to the water."

"Is this our boat?"

"Sure is, and she's the *Star Of Samoa*."

"But we live in Vermont," I said, wearing my dog harness, wondering what Soup was going to do next. Could all of this stuff amount to Soup's plan for our gift to Sinker? Or to help save Sinker's job at Station WGYP?

I had to admit that our *Star Of Samoa* actual did float. Wood usual does. The two water tanks below her deck added buoyancy.

"Wait here," said a departing Soup Vinson, "and shuck off all your clothes, and your griddles."

He returned with a length of old rope.

"I don't want to do it," I said.

"Nonsense," said Soup. "Of course you do."

Against my will, I skinned off my clothes, griddles, and harness. Soup, with his tin snips, then cut and cut and cut the black-rubber truck-tire inner tube into a very odd shape. He had rubber left over.

"What's *that?*" I asked him.

"This," he said, "is your diving suit. To keep you warm. A wet suit for wet water."

"An inner tube?"

"Right. Here, try it on. After all the favors I do for you, the least you can do is cooperate."

I tried it on. It covered some of me, certain not everything. My behind was as naked as a couple of biscuits.

"You'll adjust to it," said Soup. "Put on your dog harness and we'll be all set to go."

He, I noticed, was still clothed.

We pushed off, paddling our poker table with our hands. The water was icy cold. About a hundred feet from shore, we drifted slowly to a stop. All around us, the water looked very blue and quite deep. Looking down, however, I could see bottom. Not clearly.

Again I felt the icy water.

"We're going down *there?*" I asked Soup.

"Oh, not me. You are."

"No I'm not. Why don't *you* go?"

Soup sighed. "If it's your girl, it's your pearl. Besides, *both* of us can't go. I'm the pumper."

"What am I?"

"You," said Soup with a grin, "are a pearl diver."

"I don't want to be one."

"Yes you do. Think how Norma Jean Bissell just adores pearls. A lot more than worms."

I thought about Norma Jean Bissell. And maybe Soup Vinson was right, I was considering, as he slipped the gasoline can over my head. I could see through the plastic tray. What I saw was Soup's crazy smile, as he fastened my gas can helmet to my dog harness.

"Ready?" he asked.

"No."

Soup pointed at the water. "Down there," he said, "lies a big Black Pearl. *We,* old sport, are going to find it."

"Both of us?" I asked.

"Well," he said, "after a fashion."

"But I don't want a Black Pearl," I said.

Soup sang, "Norma Jean does."

Why I agreed to become a pearl diver I will never understand. There he was, pumping the tire pump into one of my two rotten hoses. I could hear air come hissing into my gasoline can helmet. It smelled like The Dump. As he pumped, Soup talked into *his* funnel, suspended around his neck by a wire loop, at the far end of the talking hose.

"Rob, can you hear me?" he honked.

Pressing my ear into the funnel inside my helmet, I heard Soup again asking me the same question.

"Can you hear me, Rob?"

"Yes, but I—"

"Then we're ready to dive," said Soup, "as soon as I knot this safety rope to the back of your dog harness, and also to the handle at the top of your gasoline can."

Then, ignoring my protests, Soup laced both of my sneakered feet into the army boots. Heavier now. Because he again inner-tubed the boot soles onto the tops of the stove griddles.

"The griddles will make you sink," Soup explained.

"I don't want to sink. I want to *live.*"

"Right," said Soup. "Alive or dead, the noble name of Robert Newton Peck will *live forever,* whenever the subjects of contest winners and heroic pearl diving come up."

"How do I come up?"

"I haul you up by the rope."

"Soon?"

"As soon as you locate the treasure."

"Oh."

"Ready?"

"No, I—"

My pal, my good old faithful buddy Luther Wesley Vinson, without even so much as a moving farewell ceremony, splashed me into Wet Lake.

Miss Boland had been correct.

Wet Lake is wetter.

It's colder.

Down I sank, into the shivering depths, hoping that Soup would pump me enough air. Down, down, down I went, to what I was convinced would be my frozen death.

"Pump!" I hollered.

"Are you going down?" I heard Soup ask through the hose with funnels at both ends.

"Yes."

"Have you hit bottom yet?"

"No."

I hit bottom. Or, rather, my griddles did. Clouds of sandy silt puffed up from my feet. My two griddles were probable making some very big round footprints.

"I hit bottom," I said through chattering teeth.

"Good. Find it."

"I can't seem to walk. These stove griddles are too heavy to lift down here in the mud."

"Then jump."

Bending my knees, I jumped. It sort of worked, after a fashion. I'd not jumped very far or very high. I landed again. Looking around, I couldn't see too much. The plastic tray had something smeared on the inside. Or maybe on the outside.

"Well?" honked Soup from above. "Talk to me. After all, I went to a lot of bother in order to prepare you for pearl diving. So, find us one."

I knew I'd never find it. Not even if I stayed down here a million years.

"Keep jumping," Soup said.

"Keep pumping," I said.

Water was rising. It came creeping into my gasoline can, up to my chin. Looking down in panic, I saw a fish swim by, inside my helmet. It was a crappie. And that's how I felt.

"Each time I jump," I told Soup, "my stove griddles leave big round spots. Sort of like elephant tracks."

"Perfect," said Soup, for some reason.

I jumped again and again.

Yet it was a hopeless cause. Because my plastic tray was steamy inside, making my visibility close to zero. All I did was create more elephant tracks. So I kept on jumping. Who knows, maybe I might get lucky and we'd be contest winners. If I lived.

I jumped.

Clank!

One of my metallic stove griddles hit something. Kicking it again made the same sound.

Clank!

Looking down, I couldn't see much. Bending both knees, I let myself sink, deep enough to feel. I felt it. Whatever it was, it certain was round. Blinking, I strained my eyes to look. *Holy cow!*

It was a big black ball.

I roped it. Underwater roping isn't easy, because my loop kept slipping off. Yet I wouldn't quit. I final looped it, and then yanked my lifeline. Twice. The signal for Soup to haul me up. And up I came, to climb aboard with my big black ball.

"Rob," said Soup in an impressed tone, "you really *are* a pearl of a diver. Congratulations."

"Thanks," I said. "But do not ever expect me to do it again. No matter how many pearls are down there in Wet Lake."

We were home (at Soup's house, that is) by half past four, barely in time to click on Soup's radio. To-day, we knew, would be the important announce-ment. We'd learn the name or names of the contest winner.

"Now," the announcer whispered, "here is Sinker O. Sailor to tell you all about . . . the Big Winner."

Soup and I couldn't breathe. We pressed our faces as close to the radio as we could get.

"Shipmates," said our hero, "this is Sinker O. Sailor. And we have a . . . Big Winner! In fact, we have two winners. A team of two from Learning, Vermont."

Sinker paused.

My heart stopped.

"Their names are . . . Robert and Luther."

Soup looked at me. I looked back at him. Neither of us could utter even a single word. All we did was jump to our feet and dance for a solid minute. It wasn't easy for the three of us to dance around in happy little circles.

We were carrying the radio.

11

"Places," said Miss Boland.

We were at school, but Miss Kelly wasn't in full command. Her best buddy, Miss Boland, had arrived, wearing her customary white nurse's uniform.

A song was entirely Miss Boland's idea.

Our nurse had originated an anthem, one that our entire school would sing to Mr. Sinker O. Sailor, on Sinker Day. Handing each of us a mimeograph copy of the fruits of her creative talents, Miss Boland then assembled us into a chorus.

Three rows.

Little kids in front. Larger ones behind. And the tallest ones in the back row. We all held the song words, on paper.

"I couldn't find my baton," said Miss Boland, who was now holding a toilet plunger. "For practice, this'll just have to do."

At first, I thought our nurse was kidding. But no, Miss Boland seemed to be serious—standing before us, her plunger now high in the air, as though the twenty-eight of us were a symphony orchestra.

She turned to tell Miss Kelly how happy she was that Soup and I had won the contest. The news of yesterday was all over town. Everyone seemed so glad for us.

Except for two schoolkids.

Meanwhile, my good old air-pumping pal, Soup, was whispering something to them, the two tough kids who had taken our sailing caps. Janice and Eddy weren't wearing them today. Their faces scowled with jealousy.

"Janice," I overheard Soup say, "there's an *elephant* at Wet Lake. He's still up there."

"You're a liar," snarled Janice.

"Yeah," said Eddy. "That circus elephant was a long time ago."

"Don't take my word for it," Soup told them. "Elephants live for years and years. Hike the trail up to Lonesome Mountain and see for yourself. You too, Eddy. You'll find fresh elephant tracks. Elephants have big round feet and that makes their footprints easy to spot. They're big and round too. Honest. Rob and I both saw them. We think the elephant waded into the water. We plan to swim out a ways, then dive down and look. Maybe there's tracks on the lake bottom. Rob and I heard the circus was offering a *reward*. Maybe *free tickets*."

"Let's all be quiet," said Miss Kelly, "and allow Miss Boland to plunge us into her musical magnificat."

"Ready," ordered Miss Boland, "and *begin!*"

Down came her toilet plunger.

Nothing happened.

"Are we supposed to *sing* these words?" asked Norma Jean Bissell.

"Of course," said Miss Boland. "After all, troops, what's on the paper is a *song,* isn't it?"

"I'm not sure," Soup whispered.

"Miss Boland," I asked, "what's the tune? All we have here are the words."

"Doggone it," said Miss Boland, "I knew there was a minor detail, or chord, that I overlooked. Because I was up half the night, excitedly working on the words alone. I can't believe Sinker's really coming. However, we can't let little matters like having no tune defeat us. We can make up a tune as we sing the lyric."

"How?" asked Norma Jean.

"Easy," insisted Miss Boland. "You'll just warble out whatever note you have in mind, as long as it fits my tempo. So we'll produce harmony as well as melody."

I saw Miss Kelly roll her eyes.

"Okay," said Miss Boland, once again lifting the plunger to point toward the ceiling, "here we go. *Sing!*"

We sang. Or tried to.

The words of Miss Boland's song were already dismal enough. Yet when we added twenty-eight melodies, all of them different and off-key, the end result was the most unharmonious noise I'd ever heard. We weren't a chorus. Instead, we sounded a lot closer to a factory.

"This hurts my teeth," Soup said.

Miss Kelly winced.

Miss Boland, on the other hand, a person who should have been given an honorary title of Patron Saint of the Tone-Deaf, didn't seem to notice what a dreadful din we were making. Whatever the song lacked in meter it made up in length. Miss Boland's smile widened with every agonizing verse:

> Sinker O. Sailor's come to town.
> He's now safe. His ship can't go down.
> Nobody here at him will frown.
> We're so glad that he couldn't drown.
>
> We think he's swell. His tattoo is swank.
> And on that, Sinker, you can bank.
> We're happy that your boat's not sank.
> And gladder still you're here to anchor.
>
> He has sailed the whole wide world vast.
> His adventures are not all past.
> To harbor, with a bowline knotted fast.
> His ensign flag is up his mast.

He's now ashore, instead of afloat.
And we're all happy enough to gloat.
To him, today we gladly devote.
And hope he's pleased. With a goat.

Here in Learning no typhoons whirl.
His mainsail is down. It is unfurl.
He's here to greet us, boy and girl.
Sinker O. Sailor. He's our pearl.

Not a one of us sang the same word at the same time. Or honked the same tune. It made my hair ache.

When we finally gritted and grinded to a finish, there was total silence; except for Janice, who, I'd heard, hadn't kept up with the rest of us. "He's our pearl," sang Janice in a straining soprano that must have been the result of gargling cinders. But, to be fair to Janice Riker, none of the rest of us finished on the same beat.

Turning to our teacher, Miss Boland said, "Now, you'll have to admit, you won't hear an anthem like *that* every day."

"No," said Miss Kelly. "I quite agree."

"Do you think the children know it well enough, or should we rehearse it several times more?"

Miss Kelly's answer was trigger-quick. "Oh," she told Miss Boland, "I doubt if another run-through could improve upon what I just heard." As she spoke, I saw our teacher eyeing something that always sat on her desk.

A bottle of headache tablets.

Miss Boland, for some reason, seemed pleased. "Excellent," she told us. "Remember, each and every one of you ought to memorize the words of my anthem, in order to pound it properly on Sinker Day."

To my ear, Miss Boland's creation (or creature) had already been pounded. A more accurate term might be *mangled* or *shredded*.

"What a relief," said Miss Boland, "to feel secure that my song will be singable. I've still got a list of preparations a mile long."

"I'll bet you have," said Miss Kelly. "So it would hardly be fair of us to tarry you here, rehearsing the . . . the *music*."

Miss Kelly moved a step toward the door.

"Right," said Miss Boland.

We waited.

Perhaps it was sort of like being in church. Everyone praying a silent prayer, one that pleaded for not having to whack out Miss Boland's anthem again. Now, or ever.

"Say," said our nurse, the plunger held in her armpit like a British officer's swagger stick, "I plumb forgot."

"About what?" asked Miss Kelly. "It isn't another verse of your anthem, is it?"

Miss Boland shook her head, then looked a bit puzzled. "Do you think the five verses I wrote will be adequate, or should I rush home and write five more?"

"*No,*" said Miss Kelly. "Believe me, the five verses we heard are *more than enough.*"

"Good," said Miss Boland.

Turning toward the door, our nurse pulled a long white slip of paper from the side pocket of her white uniform. "What I forgot was this. To round up a few volunteers. For example, I'll have to collar two people"—Miss Boland held up two chubby fingers—"to escort Mr. Sinker O. Sailor to The Thumb, where our celebration picnic is to be held."

Soup nudged me.

"Quit it," I told him.

Miss Boland glanced at Soup and me. "Hmmm," she hummed, "perhaps it would be fitting if Luther and Robert, our contest winners, could handle this for us. Would you, please?"

Soup stood up.

"We'd be glad to, Miss Boland."

He sat.

"Perfect," said our nurse. "But please don't just go and collect Sinker, then lug him to the picnic as though he's an everyday citizen. This, after all, is his special event. Sinker Day. And he's to be our guest of honor."

I looked confused.

"Think up a way," said Miss Boland, "to bring Mr. Sinker O. Sailor to The Thumb, so he'll arrive as a sailor should."

"Navy style?" Soup asked her.

"*Yes,*" said Miss Boland, gesturing enthusiastically

with her plunger. "But I haven't got the time to think up just *how.*" She stuffed the duty list back into her pocket. "Just see that Sinker arrives at the picnic. In style. As you suggested, Luther, a seagoing idea would be in keeping. Something *naval.*"

Janice Riker pointed at her belly button.

Miss Kelly reached for the Anacin.

12

"Hurry," said Soup.

It was after school. The two of us stood at The Dump again. Why, I didn't know.

"Soup," I said, "whatever you're planning, I'm never taking another pearl dive."

"No," said Soup, "you're not. What we have to do now is prepare a surprise for Mr. Sinker O. Sailor. We're going to improve our lovely lady."

"Is that Miss Boland?" I asked.

"Not quite," Soup told me.

"Who?"

"*Star Of Samoa,*" said Soup. "Rob, just wait until you see what our little raft is going to become. And how *fast* she'll go."

"It doesn't have an engine," I said.

"Not yet," said Soup, with a sly smirk.

"Is this some sort of a prank?"

"Of course not," said Soup, as he began his frantic search, throwing junk one way, then another. "Luck is with us, Rob. After all, we found the Black Pearl, raised it, hoisted it aboard the *Star Of Samoa,* and brought it to shore."

"Safely hidden," I said, thinking of how rapturously I yearned to give our Black Pearl to Norma Jean Bissell. A befitting token that would endear me to her forever.

Soup, in a frenzy, was diving into piles of rubbish as though it were department store merchandise and we were millionaires.

"Ah," said Soup, "I found one."

I looked.

Soup was holding a snow shovel. "Rob," he said, "hustle up and dig down. Because we'll be needing *two.*"

Naturally, I was thinking. On a warm sunny day in May, how could we hope to get by with only one snow shovel? I sighed, realizing my infection was becoming complete. I'd caught it. Rob Peck was now as nutty as Soup Vinson.

"Never mind," said Soup. "I found another."

There he stood, smiling broadly, clutching a snow shovel in each hand, perhaps anticipating a blizzard.

"Find a chisel or a crowbar, Rob. While you're at

it, yank a big shirtful of stuffing out of that cruddy old mattress you're standing on."

"Why?"

"You'll soon discover, old top, so pitch in."

I did what Soup requested.

Soup let out a war whoop. "Yaa-hoooooo!"

Carrying an armful of mattress stuffing that smelled worse than Miss Boland's anthem, I ran to see what Soup had uncovered.

"There it is," said Soup.

"A seesaw?"

All it was, as far as I could see, was a long wooden plank. In the middle, equidistant from the two ends, there was a hole, about baseball size.

"Here," said Soup, "are the two metal stanchions that support it. We're all set."

I looked down at a pair of long-legged croquet wickets, formed out of thick pipe bent into two curves.

"Perfect," said Soup, "because with *two* stanchions, our mast pole can swing back and forth."

"Goody," I said in disdain, totally baffled as to why our poker table needed a teeter-totter. Or a pair of snow shovels.

Collecting what Soup required, we started uphill once again, toward Wet Lake. I prayed this would be our final trek. But would it be? Probable not. My dread was that, for the rest of my life, I'd have to lug and tug every discarded doodad up Lonesome Mountain.

In our town, The Dump would be there no longer. Every hunk of junk would soon be at Wet Lake.

Rob Peck and Soup Vinson, I feared, would reside up yonder, forever, assembling goofy gadgets. All of them eventual to be used for self-destruction.

We arrived at the lake.

I was sweaty and exhausted. Soup, on the other hand, seemed charged with the renewed energy of a robot.

"Rob," he said, tossing me a hatchet, "we need a beanpole, ten feet long, and thick enough to jam more than halfway up through the center of our seesaw. Thin end up."

Instead of asking why, I just did it.

Soup busied himself with a chisel. Measuring carefully, he chipped four holes in the tabletop. In the middle, he gouged a slit about a yard or so long. As he worked, he whistled merrily and mumbled something about *elephant tracks.*

"Now what?" I asked the mad scientist.

"Now," Soup told me, "we create."

Working together, we jammed the pair of two-legged wicket-shaped stanchions into the four holes in the deck. Between the stanchions ran Soup's long new slit. Three inches wide.

Over the slit, Soup nailed a long strip of black rubber, cut from our old inner tube. A slit also ran the length of the rubber strip, or almost.

"What's the slit in the deck for, Soup?"

"Oh," he said, "that's to allow our mast to wiggle back and forth. The rest," said Soup, "won't be easy."

We rolled the poker-table raft to the lake's edge and floated it in the shallow shore water.

We took off all our clothes.

Just in case.

Our next step was to place the long teeter-totter plank on its two stanchions, the wickets. Then we installed the ten-foot pole *up* through the slit in the center of the deck, between the stanchions, through the hole in the middle of the seesaw plank, and up into the air for six feet.

"Soup," I said, shivering in the cold water of Wet Lake, as the *Star Of Samoa* lay on her side, "our mast only sticks up six feet from the bottom of the deck. It'll be stabbing four feet down into the water."

Soup nodded.

"You'll see, Rob. All we do now is wire the snow shovels together, curved sides in. Hump to hump."

This we did.

"Now," said Soup, "we attach our shovels to the shorter *wet* end of our beanpole, our mast."

"What for?" I asked.

"Flippers."

"I don't get it, Soup."

"Patience. You're in for a shocker. While I'm adjusting these snow shovels, get over the topside of the deck and jam mattress stuffing into every loosely filled hole."

"Why?"

"So our boat doesn't take a leak!" said Soup.

I did it.

"Now," said Soup, as we flipped the crazy craft right again, "she still floats. The tanks of air sure do help. One final touch, Rob, and we're ready to test her."

Soup stood on the center of the seesaw and tied our little Samoa flag to the dry end of the mast, six feet above the deck.

We both saluted.

"Ready?" Soup asked me.

We were still naked and shivering, but my burning curiosity was keeping me fairly warm.

We tested.

It didn't work.

"Cheer up," Soup told me. "I've located our problem. Trouble is, I can't figure out how to solve it."

"What's the problem?"

"See?" said Soup. "One of our stanchions is loose. It's too rickety. So we can't seesaw up and down with any thrust power."

"It needs something," I said.

Furthermore, I knew exactly what. Splashing to shore, I went to find a hidden object, then returned to the shallow water and our craft.

"Rob," said Soup, "you can't be serious."

"We'll see," I told him.

Without more explanation, I wedged my bright idea (the object) under the loose stanchion, between its two legs.

"There," I said. "Ready to test."

We tried it once again.

Our teeter-totter was sideways to the direction we wanted our vessel to move. On the ends of our see-saw, Soup and I didn't face forward and backward. We faced each other, so both he and I could look dead ahead; Soup looked over his right shoulder, I over my left.

"Here goes, Rob," said Soup.

He went up, while I went down. Up, down, up, down. As we pumped, the beanpole mast began to swing in the air, left and right. Beneath the deck, the short end of the mast (I presumed) moved the horizontal snow shovels. Our flippers.

The *Star Of Samoa* chugged forward.

Not rapidly. Yet she moved.

"It works," said Soup.

"Wow," I said, as our knots increased.

"Rob," said Soup, as the two of us, jaybird-naked, seesawed the *Star Of Samoa* out into Wet Lake, "thar she goes because of *you,* old tiger. You solved our rickety problem."

From my momentary high position on our teeter-totter, I glanced down at what I'd wedged between the wicket legs.

A Black Pearl.

13

Saturday came.

"Rob," said Soup, "today is our big day."

Indeed. It was Sinker Day.

Following our chores, Soup and I raced to The Thumb, the little peninsula of land inside the horseshoe bend of the crick.

Arriving, I couldn't believe what I saw.

All of the rectangular picnic tables had been positioned end to end, like a freight train. And there stood Miss Boland, hanging colorful streamers of blue and white on the edges of the *one picnic table,* which was longer than two bowling alleys.

Miss Boland was in uniform.

But not as a nurse.

Instead, she was decked out as a sailor. On her head perched something that was trying to be a homemade Sinker O. Sailor cap. A white navy admiral's costume, gold-fringed epaulets on each shoulder, and more gold stripes on her sleeves than had been awarded to either John Paul Jones or Lord Nelson. Several medals were pinned on her tunic, above a pocket, and below. Around her waist ran a lengthy blue sash, complete with a brass telescope at one hip. At her other hip, a sword.

Her boots were blue, with silvery spangles.

Turning, she spotted us, smiled, and rewarded Soup and me with a snappy salute.

"Aye, aye, me hearties, 'tis I," said Miss Boland. "Do I look nautical, or just naughty?"

Soup and I nodded, not trusting ourselves to comment.

People arrived. Mostly in families. Several small children pointed at Miss Boland, asking their parents if she was Sinker O. Sailor or Moby Dick. A few wore white sailing caps. I looked around for the two tough kids who had stolen ours, Janice Riker and Eddy Tacker.

They weren't there.

Their absence made me worry, and begin to wonder what those two rotters were up to.

The Learning High School Marching Band appeared, all in green, toting their assorted brass weapons of musical destruction. Then came a color guard of four men, the Sons of Ethan Allen. Next, our American Legion Drill Team, locally known as The Out-of-Steppers. I saw a troop of Camp Fire Kids, Brownies, plus our town baseball team in their all-wool summer game suits.

Miss Gibbons came too. Very slowly.

She was an elderly lady who always carried an umbrella (rain or shine) and constantly recited *The Boy Stood on the Burning Deck,* rarely by request.

Along came our local fire department, The Learning Volunteer Flamers, astride the community's only red pumper. As the truck attempted a sharp curve, and failed, several firemen (known for their fondness for firewater) fell off.

Everyone in town was here.

Except for one particular person.

"I wonder," Miss Boland wondered, "what could be keeping our special guest of honor?"

A blink later, another truck arrived at the picnic. Not a red one. This was a truck none of us had seen before. It was larger than our fire engine, and pure white. Large letters had been painted on its massive side:

WGYP

"Ahoy," Miss Boland exclaimed, dropping her blue and white bunting. "He's here. But I had no idea he'd come in a truck."

We all surged forward, eager to get our very first close-up peek at a genuine honest-to-gosh celebrity. The large rear door of the WGYP vehicle slowly dropped open, to reveal a stage, microphones, and strange black boxes, all of which sprouted dozens of wires and cables.

With curiosity, Miss Boland eyed the large WGYP truck, now open, and becoming active.

"You don't suppose," she asked Soup and me, "that they might plan to put on some sort of a radio show, do you? I wonder whose idea that was."

Soup glanced quickly at me, a warning finger to his lips, coupled with a slight shake of his head.

A man appeared.

"There he is!" a local citizen shouted.

The man on the truck's tailgate smiled, then shook his head. "No," he said, "I'm hardly the star. All I am is just one of the crew. A sound technician. My job is to set up a loudspeaker so you folks can hear the radio program."

"Did . . . Sinker come?" asked Soup.

The technician nodded. "You bet. Don't fret."

I saw Miss Boland sigh.

"Where is he?" people wanted to know.

"Oh," the man explained, "he's around . . . some-where. But remember, Sinker O. Sailor is a shy gent, so please don't stampede all over him. Until he's ready. Okay?"

"Okay," we mumbled.

"Besides," the technician warned us, "I believe that our radio star might be making sort of a surprise entrance. He'll be holding a small portable microphone."

Before anyone else could say another word, Miss Boland hustled Soup and me to one side.

"Luther and Robert," she instructed, "it's your job to sneak Sinker away from here, and pronto. Then, after the band plays *Anchors Aweigh,* and before Mayor Doolittle speaks, make your grand entrance. And remember, Sinker is a sailor, so *don't bring him by land.*"

"No," said Soup. "Rob and I have it all worked out."

"We do?" I asked Soup.

If so, it was news to me.

"We'll bring him that way," Soup said, pointing at the smooth crick water. "Okay?"

"Splendid," said Miss Boland. "Go fetch Sinker. He's probable up front, in the cab. So sneak him away quick, and then make sure his entrance is fast, and dramatic, and a *surprise.*"

Soup winked.

"Oh, we will, Miss Boland," he said.

We hurried away.

Sure enough, in the front of the truck, there sat our hero, Mr. Sinker O. Sailor, in sailing togs. I'd expected a large, muscular man with a ruddy, salt-whipped complexion. As he dismounted, I saw that

Sinker was short, slender, and pale. He had very white hair.

"Mr. Sinker," said Soup, "here we are. My name is Luther Vinson, and this is my friend."

"Sir," I said, "I'm Robert Peck."

"Oh"—he brightened—"you're the two fine lads that wrote us such a persuasive letter. I'm very pleased to meet both of you." Smiling warmly, he extended a frail but friendly hand. In his other hand, Sinker held something like a large lollipop.

"What's that?" Soup asked him.

"This? Oh, it's a new-fangled thing, a wireless microphone, so we can broadcast a special Saturday morning radio show to all our listeners." He nodded at the truck. "Our sound truck picks up whatever the three of us say, when the time comes, and then it's transmitted to the WGYP audience."

"Whatever *we* say?" Soup asked. "You mean Rob and I are going to be on the *radio*? Just like *you?*"

Sinker nodded.

"Yes," he said gently. "You boys are my Big Winners. And today, WGYP is broadcasting a live show, with real hometown people. Just as you boys suggested in your letter."

I gulped. "Honest?"

"Indeed so," said Sinker. "Today *you lads* are the WGYP radio stars. Not me."

"Hurry," said Soup. "Please follow us. Rob and I

113

have the honor of helping you make your dramatic entrance."

"Let's go," said Sinker O. Sailor. "Lead the way."

He followed us, carrying his little wireless microphone, up the long winding trail, the entire way to Wet Lake. It was a quick trip, as, for once, we weren't carrying part of The Dump.

"Say," he said, "this is a roundabout route."

"It's part of your surprise, sir," said Soup.

It was also my surprise, because whatever my pal was planning was a mystery to me.

We stopped. Sinker pointed at our little floating vessel, his face contorted in confusion. "What . . . *What is it?*"

"*She,*" said Soup proudly, "is transportation, sir."

"*Star Of Samoa,*" I said.

"A boat?" Sinker asked us.

"We knew you'd be pleased, sir," Soup said. "It's a present. Rob and I made it ourselves. Just for you."

"Thank you, boys. It's . . . It's . . .well, you don't see a ship like that every day. I'm very grateful." He looked at his watch. "Now, perhaps we ought to be strolling back down to the picnic. Because, wherever I am at *noon,* that's when we start broadcasting our first Saturday radio program."

"Excellent," said Soup, wading into the shallow water, waving a hand for Sinker to board our boat. "Let's go, sir."

"On . . . On *that?*"

Sinker O. Sailor's face seemed to be turning even paler. Color drained from his cheeks. He looked at the lake. "That's a lot of *water* out there," he said, "for this little boat."

"Aye," said Soup.

"I don't see an engine," Sinker said, "or a sail."

"Don't worry, sir," I said. "Soup and I will man the mechanical duties. I mean the seesaw. You only have to be our idle passenger."

"Soup?" he asked. "Who is Soup?"

Soup grinned. "My real name's Luther, but I'm sort of partial to Soup, as Robert here can tell you."

"Rob," I said informally, "for short."

"Soup and Rob?" he asked.

"Aye, aye," we smartly replied.

Looking at his watch, Sinker raised his eyebrows by an inch. "Oh," he said, "it's almost noon. When the little red light flashes on my microphone, no matter what, we'll be broadcasting."

"Time to shove off, sir," said Soup. "Sorry that your ankles and pant legs are getting wet." Soup laughed. "But after all the oceans you've conquered, what's a few quarts of Wet Lake?"

Holding his nose, Mr. Sinker climbed aboard the *Star Of Samoa* and then immediately closed his eyes. Perhaps it was some seagoing custom I hadn't heard about.

Soup and I shoved off.

"How . . . How deep is it here?" asked Sinker.

"Oh," I said, "we apologize for that, sir. Because you're so used to deep ocean water, fathoms and fathoms, that our little old pond won't be deep enough for a seagoer like yourself. Here, it's only ten feet deep."

"Ten feet?"

"Sorry, sir," said Soup. "We know that to you, ten feet is disgustingly shallow. But don't get bored, sir, because soon we'll be over a depth of twenty feet."

"That's right, sir," I said. "For your pleasure, we'll sort of steer for the deepest part of Wet Lake."

Sinker moaned.

Eyes closed, our passenger was gripping one of the seesaw stanchion legs, his face changing color again. White to green.

As Soup and I pumped up and down on the teeter-totter, our unseen horizontal snow shovels swished. Forward lurched our good ship *Star Of Samoa,* toward the bluer and deeper and wetter waters of Wet Lake. A gallon or two sloshed across the deck with every pump, repeatedly soaking our hero. Was he uncomfortable? That, I decided, was absurd. He was a seasoned sailor.

Sinker's hands, moving to seek a firmer hold, found the wedge, our treasured round thing I'd used to tighten the seesaw stanchion so it wouldn't be rickety.

"What's *this?*" asked Sinker, opening his eyes.

"That," said Soup, pumping up and down, "is what Rob found on the bottom of the lake, and we salvaged it. It's a pearl."

Sinker blinked. His mouth fell open.

116

"My . . . my Black Pearl."

"*Yours?*" I asked.

"Yes, of course it's mine. There's only one like it. It's my treasure. Years ago, I lost it in this lake. My bowling ball."

"*A bowling ball?*" Soup and I said in unison.

Sinker nodded. "I invented it. You see, it's the only bowling ball in America with no holes."

"We thought it was a Black Pearl," I said.

"That's what I called it," said Sinker, "because I was never without it. My lucky charm. It was a mistake to take it out in a rowboat. Ever since I tipped and lost it in the lake, I've hated water."

"If your bowling ball had no holes," Soup asked, "how could you hold it, in order to roll it?"

Sinker smiled. "With both hands."

A bowling ball, I thought. How could I give an old bowling ball to Norma Jean Bissell? Even one with no holes. Besides, it wasn't mine to give. It belonged to Sinker O. Sailor.

"When I bowled with it," Sinker bragged, "I couldn't miss. I became so good a bowler with my holeless ball that the other bowlers complained. Then the A.B.A., the American Bowlers Association, ruled my ball illegal."

"Illegal?" I echoed.

Sinker nodded sadly, his hand patting his treasured ball. "Yes," he said. "I'll never forget that headline on the front page of the *Gutter Gazette*."

"What did the headline say?" asked Soup.

117

Sinker sighed. " 'No Holes Barred.' "

The *Star Of Samoa* wasn't sinking. Only my heart. I had no special pearl for Norma Jean.

Sinker looked ahead, still holding his microphone.

"Where," he asked us, "are we headed?"

"To the foot of the lake," said Soup. "That'll be the fork where the waters divide. We follow the crick to the picnic area."

"Is the water deep here?" asked Sinker.

"Yes," I said, guessing, in an effort to please our honorable guest with deep water. "It's the deepest part of the lake."

Sinker's face turned from green to ashen.

"Boys," he said, "I'm so afraid."

Soup flinched. So did I.

"*You?*" we asked. "But you're Sinker O. Sailor."

"I'm a fake," Sinker confessed. "A phony. All I am is a radio voice. The only thing real about me is my tattoo. For years, since I tipped over, I haven't set foot on a boat. Nor have I ever even *seen* an ocean. I'm scared to death in a bathtub. I only take showers. Water terrifies me so much that I have to drink it from a spoon!"

"Honest?" Soup asked.

"Yes," said Sinker. "And I'll tell you one more secret."

We waited. And our hero told us.

"I can't swim."

14

"Don't worry," Soup told Sinker.

"Sir," I added, "Soup and I want to be more than fans. We're your friends. And we won't tell anybody that you can't swim."

"But," said Soup, as our *Star Of Samoa* tipped a bit, "we hope you're a quick learner."

As the two of us pumped up and down on the see-saw plank, our poker-table boat surged forward.

Opening an eye, Sinker checked his wristwatch.

"Oh, golly gee," he gasped. "It's noon." A little red light flashed on his microphone. "Ahoy, little ship-mates," he said to it. "This is Sinker O. Sailor. Where am I? Well, I'm aboard ship." His voice cracked. "Away out on the deep waters of Wet Lake, near Learning,

Vermont . . . aboard the good ship *Star Of Samoa*."

Soup and I, working our teeter-totter up and down, grinned at each other. *We were on the radio!* And I was secretly hoping that Norma Jean Bissell was listening, back at the picnic, where WGYP had provided a loudspeaker for the local crowd.

"Our first Saturday on-location program," said Sinker, "is brought to you by . . . by . . ." His hand briefly covered the microphone. "I forgot the name of that stuff."

"Soggymushies," whispered Soup.

"Soggymushies," said Sinker, "your favorite breakfast cereal and mine. With me, here on the *Star Of Samoa*, are my two Big Winners of the radio contest . . . Luther Wesley Vinson and Robert Newton Peck."

My chest swelled.

"And," said Sinker, "the three of us are the only ones here on Wet Lake, on our way to a picnic."

But right then, I suddenly realized that today would be *no picnic*. What I saw at that moment curdled my blood as well as my breakfast.

We weren't alone on Wet Lake!

Trouble was headed our way. Double trouble. From the rear, two people in a canoe were approaching the stern of our *Star Of Samoa*. Both of them appeared to be blue. Quite blue. Except for their faces, which were red with rage.

Soup saw them too.

120

"Oh, *no*," he said to me. "It's Janice and Eddy."

Janice Riker and Eddy Tacker, wearing our white sailing caps, were gaining on us. And paddling fast.

"Rob!" yelled Soup, "seesaw for your life."

"Somebody's coming," said Sinker. "And I bet they're two more people to join the . . . the fun."

"No," said Soup. "They're pirates."

"Pirates?" asked Sinker. "Here on Wet Lake?"

"Right, sir," I said. "Those two swabs took our caps away from us. And now, maybe they want to take *you*."

"*Me?*" asked Sinker.

"Pump!" hollered Soup. "Pump faster, Rob."

We pumped.

"The pirates are gaining on us," Sinker said. "Are they really mean pirates?"

"The meanest," Soup and I replied.

"Pirates," said Sinker to the microphone. "A pair of angry-looking pirates are closing in on our ship."

"We're gonna tip you over," snarled Janice.

"Yeah," said Eddy, "into deep water."

"Did you hear that?" Sinker O. Sailor asked the microphone. "We'll all drown."

"Rob," said Soup, "keep on pumping."

We pumped. The pirates gained. Now their canoe was almost close enough to reach the *Star Of Samoa*.

"Why are you pirates so angry?" Sinker asked them.

"Because," said Janice, "we couldn't find any elephant. All we found were a lot of dumb old elephant tracks. And we're both about froze to death in that icy water."

Eddy pointed at our bowling ball.

"Hey," he said. "You got the Black Pearl!"

"Yeah," growled Janice, "and we want it."

"You heard the voices of those horrible pirates," Sinker told the microphone. "They are after our treasure . . . the Black Pearl."

"Hand it over," Eddy threatened. "Or else!"

"No way," Soup said, and turned to Sinker. "Sir, it's your prize possession. You just recovered it after years of being sadly without it. The secret of Wet Lake, the Black Pearl, is yours."

"Shipmates," our hero told us, "you are the bravest of the brave. Thank you, Robert and Luther, for your loyalty to your captain and your ship. So I'm rewarding the pair of you."

"How?" asked Soup.

To Janice and Eddy, Sinker said, "A truce. If you pirates return those two white sailing caps to Soup and Rob, then, and only then, will I give you my Black Pearl, in trade."

To my surprise, Janice and Eddy tossed us our sailing caps. We caught them.

"Now," said Janice, "we want the Black Pearl."

"Here comes," said Sinker O. Sailor. "Catch it."

A bowling ball isn't light. Yet up it arced, a high two-handed delivery. Down it fell. Janice reached. So

did Eddy. But a slippery wet bowling ball isn't easily caught by two dumb, clumsy pirates who are attempting to stand up in a bobbing canoe.

They missed it.

KA-SPLOOOSH-GURGLE-BLUB.

Black Pearl sank. The canoe tipped.

"Oops," said Janice.

"This isn't good," said Eddy, about to lose his dry wit.

Into the wet waters of Wet Lake splashed a couple of capless and hapless pirates. Best of all, Sinker O. Sailor described the joyful event to our radio audience.

"Soup and Rob," he commanded us in a take-charge tone, "man the pump. Or rather, boy the seesaw. Our proud ship *Star Of Samoa* is now safely coming about, and picnicbound."

Soup and I cheered.

"Thanks a lot, sir," Soup said.

"You saved us, Mr. Sinker," I told him. "You really are a genuine *hero!*" I said it in my loudest voice, so our radio audience would salute Sinker O. Sailor's pluck.

"And," hollered Soup, "I love Soggymushies!"

"So does Buttinski," I added.

Without being asked, Sinker helped hold the rickety stanchion (which formerly had been steadied by the Black Pearl) in place, allowing Soup and me to pump the teeter-totter. From here on, our voyage to the picnic location, The Thumb, would be a spanking breeze. Norma Jean Bissell would be there, viewing my triumphant arrival. Then I'd modestly tell her how (almost single-handed) I outfoxed the pesky pirates of the high sea. Well, maybe the high lake.

Our troubles were over.

As Soup and I pumped up and down, Sinker was describing the scenic beauty of Wet Lake, via Station WGYP, to back-home radio listeners.

"Say," he asked Soup and me, "what's that noise? It sounds like rushing water."

"Oh," said Soup, "that's up ahead. It's where the water laps the shore of that island where Wet Lake divides."

"Which fork do we take?" Sinker asked.

"The picnic fork," I giggled.

Sinker said, "I meant port or starboard. It's been years since I've visited Wet Lake. But, as I recall, one fork leads to Suicide Flume."

The watery noise seemed to increase.

"Good," said Soup, "we're moving faster."

Soup was right. The *Star Of Samoa* floated along with little or no help from our seesaw above the deck and our twin snow-shovel flippers below.

"The island," Sinker O. Sailor said to the microphone, "seems to be bearing a lot closer."

It was.

Soup and Sinker were looking dead ahead. So was I. But then, for some reason, I looked back over my shoulder.

Bad news.

Janice Riker and Eddy Tacker had somehow managed to right their overturned canoe and regain their paddles, and were once again pursuing us. They looked wet, cold, and angry. Soup and I had our sailing caps. Janice and Eddy had no Black Pearl. This, I concluded in a split second, could add up to only one conclusion:

Janice and Eddy were now more ornery than they were when they couldn't find the circus elephant. Only my stove griddle tracks.

"Say," said Sinker, as he pointed ahead to the island, "there's a person, standing at the water's edge. Somebody's fishing."

I looked.

Sure enough, a lonely fisherman stood on the island shore, where the waters of Wet Lake divided. As we floated closer, I saw that it was a lady wearing rubber waders and holding a fishing pole, ankle-deep in the shallows.

"Ahoy," yelled Sinker. "Ho!"

In friendly reply, the lady waved her pole.

"Which way should we go?" Sinker asked her, as we moved closer. "To the port or the starboard? We want to avoid *Suicide Flume*." He yelled the last two words.

The lady pointed.

"Ho," said Soup, "we turn to the port."

"Or," I said, forgetting which was which, "maybe it's to the starboard."

Sinker's face became suddenly sober. "It doesn't matter," he said. "Because there's something you boys forgot to add when you constructed the *Star Of Samoa*."

"What did we forget?" Soup asked.

"A steering rudder."

15

The fishing lady smiled at us.

"Say," she said, "that's quite a peculiar boat. And I see you have a *star aboard*. Howdy, Mr. Sinker."

"Hear that?" I asked Soup. "We don't go to the port. I think she said to the *starboard*."

"Turn," said Soup.

"How?" I asked him.

"Here," he said, leaping off his end of the seesaw. "We'll use *you* for a rudder."

"*Me?*"

"Hurry, Rob. We don't have time to argue. So hang on to our stern and jump into the water."

Why I agreed to be a rudder I will never really know. Except, of course, to save Sinker as well as his radio program. The water of Wet Lake was wetter (and colder) here than at the place where I'd served as a reluctant pearl diver. And behind me, Janice and Eddy were bound to catch us. A pirate is no picnic.

Sinker O. Sailor looked at me, sighed, and asked, "Why, oh why, didn't I stick to bowling?"

"Ho!" yelled Soup. "We're final turning."

"No!" shouted the fish lady.

"Good," said Soup to Sinker, "she's hollering *ho* too."

"But why," Sinker O. Sailor asked, "is she jumping up and down, and waving her arms in alarm?"

As we floated by the island, I could see her as I was ruddering. She seemed to be hysterical about something, and I could have sworn she was yelling something about Suicide Flume. It was probable not important. Nothing else could happen to us. Not with Sinker O. Sailor aboard and Soup in command.

Soup?

This, I decided, was no time to be a rudder. And our *Star Of Samoa* was now moving almost too rapidly for me to maintain my slippery grip on the stern edge of the poker table. With a mighty heave, I pulled myself up onto our poop deck, to join Sinker and Soup.

"Goodness," said Sinker, "we're going a bit fast."

Soup grinned. "Oh, that's okay. It only means we'll get to the picnic that much quicker. And we can keep ahead of the pirates."

"All is well," Sinker said to his microphone and our

audience out in Radioland. "We're picnicbound." Yet his voice sounded anything but convincing.

Our hero gripped his microphone with one hand, clinging to our beanpole mast with the other. At the peak of the mast, our little flag of Samoa, which earlier had limply sagged, was now horizontal, which proved only one fact.

We were going a lot faster.

As Sinker described our increasing knots to WGYP, I noticed that he had closed his eyes. Very tightly. But, trooper that he was, he knew the show must go on. There was a lot more bravery in Sinker than WGYP realized. To me, his age didn't matter.

"Ahead of us," Sinker O. Sailor was now saying, "the water is no longer blue. It seems to have become foamy white."

Even my pal looked worried.

"Rob," he asked me, "did that lady advise us to steer to the starboard or to the port?"

"Starboard," I answered, "as I recall."

Soup made a wry face. "Let's think," said Soup. "Is that right, or left?"

We asked Sinker.

His expression became blank. A shrug of his shoulders told me that *he* didn't know either. But then his face brightened.

"Boys," he said, "it's time to reveal my secret tattoo."

Soup and I couldn't breathe. At last, I was thinking, I'd be able to catch a personal peep at one of the closest-guarded secrets in all celebrity. I would actual see Sinker O. Sailor's tattoo!

Yanking up his shirt, Sinker bared his chest to Soup Vinson and Rob Peck.

"Okay," he told us, "there it is. But, because to *my* eyes it's upside down, I can't read it. I had it printed on my chest because I could never remember its message."

Soup read it aloud:

"Port Left.
Starboard Right."

"I'll be swamped," said Sinker. "I could have *sworn* it was the other way around."

"Maybe," gulped Soup, "we made a minor mistake, back yonder, and took the wrong fork."

Our knots increased.

"We," observed Sinker, "are now hissing with haste." He pointed to our mast flag, our little Samoa ensign, which was now whipping in the wind of our speed.

"Don't worry," said Soup. "Both streams will carry us down to The Thumb, our picnic area."

But then I looked upstream. As though we weren't in trouble enough, a canoe was being paddled our way, and in a powerful hurry. Janice and Eddy wanted revenge. Here we were. Behind us, pirates. Ahead of us, nothing but a narrowing channel of bubbling white water.

"I want to get off," said Soup.

"Me too," I told him.

"Avast," said Sinker. "Shame on both of you," he yelled above the sound of roaring water. "This is no time to desert a sinking poker table."

"Are we sinking?" I asked.

"No." Soup grinned. "She's going too fast to sink."

With no rudder, the *Star Of Samoa* seemed to possess an evil will of her own, spinning in circles, around and around as we moved along in a strengthening current.

Sinker pointed. "We're heading for a rock."

KA-BONK-BUMP.

Star Of Samoa catapulted into the air. Then she fell with a flat splash. Too flat.

"Soup," I yelped, "we lost her tanks."

My pal giggled. "Sailing," he said, "is a tankless job."

The water became not only faster but rougher. We were bobbing along as helplessly as a cork. No rudder, no sail, no engine. Heading for what appeared to be steeper rapids.

"I think," I overheard Sinker O. Sailor groan, "I know why they are called *rapids*. And I'm afraid, boys, we are headed toward . . . What was the name of that flume?"

"Suicide," said Soup.

Our deck, once a poker table at The Knights of

Saint Bingo, now spun as madly as a roulette wheel. I sighed. With good old Luther Vinson, my life was a gamble.

Vision was a blur. So was Vinson.

As we spun, I saw land, water, land, water . . . and sometimes a pursuing canoe. For me, there was no safety, no haven, either ahead or behind.

"Ahead!" shouted Sinker, "there's a waterfall."

"It'll be fun," said Soup Vinson, buoy lunatic. "So cheer up. A flume isn't a waterfall. Falls go down. But a flume only *slants* downward, at a steep angle."

White, sudsy water continued to slosh across our deck. The water, freshly flowing down from Wet Lake, was very wet. And very cold.

"Oh," mumbled Sinker to his microphone, "I've always dreamed of dying dry."

The three of us now huddled together in the exact center of our poker table, tight to the beanpole mast, clinging to what little hope (none) we could muster. Looking upward, in fervent reverence, all I could see was a fluttering Samoa flag.

"Rob," said Soup, "I forgive you."

"Forgive *me?*"

"Yes," he said. "I forgive you for failing to talk me out of ever wanting to be a sailor."

We tore down Suicide Flume. Ahead lay a waiting death. Behind, only Janice and Eddy, either of whom could pound me to a pulp with a single punch. I spotted the bottom of the flume. To me, it looked like the lower lip of a ski jumper's takeoff ramp.

The *Star Of Samoa* bucked.

"We're going to capsize," Sinker commented to me, not too dryly. "Will we capsize? Capsize? *Capsize?*"

"Small," I said.

16

Small.

That's how I felt.

Small and helpless and tiny. In fact, wee.

"Whheeeeeeee!" hollered Soup, as the *Star Of Samoa* (in the shape of a very large poker chip) took off at the foot of the flume. Through the air we flew, a giant Frisbee, turning around and around. As we three clung to the beanpole, Soup Vinson was whooping with joy.

Something else, believe it or not, was also flying through the air. Moving even faster. Passing us.

It looked like a bullet. Or a canoe.

"Soup," I said, "*do* something. Before I throw up."

So he did. He whistled nine little toots.

... − − − ...
S.O.S.

"Save Our Ship!" cried Sinker.

I remembered the name, and the initials, of our vessel. *Star Of Samoa*. Perhaps, after all, we might survive. Maybe, for Soup and me, S.O.S. was a symbol of good luck.

But then I remembered Buttinski . . . and Serve Our Soggymushies.

I prayed we'd slow to a halt, but no such luck seemed in store. As our poker chip sailed lower and lower, we started to skim across the crick, at incredible knottage. Touching water, we'd skip up again, and again, in a series of little bounces. We were spinning around so fast that I couldn't make out where we were. But then I learned.

Dead ahead, there it was. The Thumb.

"Soup," I said, "we're going to the *picnic!*"

"That," he said, "was my plan."

For a second or two, our *Star Of Samoa* stopped acting like a Frisbee. She quit spinning. Ahead, I saw faces. Their eyebrows were all raised and their mouths hung open in some sort of collective silent scream.

Water splashed me again and again. Never in my life had I been so bathed, or so showered.

Add to that frequent waves of nausea.

We skipped once more, as would a flat stone,

bouncing higher, over the panicky people. Their mouths were open, yet nobody uttered a word.

Perhaps the good citizens of Learning had never seen a flying poker table before, one bearing three very wet sailors, a beanpole mast, and a flag of Samoa.

"Ahoy!" yelled Soup.

People ducked.

Lower we glided, lower, and lower. Before us stretched our landing strip. There it was, perfectly lined up with our flight path. And quite long.

It was the picnic table.

Just as we reached it, I saw hot dogs and catsup and mustard and relish, plus countless cups of root beer. I could also make out neat little stacks of paper napkins.

And a cake.

"We're going to crash," I said.

"Yes," said Soup, "but not into *water.*"

Sinker said, "Thank the goodness."

Closing my eyes, I hung on to Soup, to the beanpole, to my sailing cap, and to Mr. Sinker O. Sailor, who was about to do what Miss Boland had requested.

Make a dramatic entrance.

The *Star Of Samoa* touched down.

To be more accurate, she skidded the entire length of a very long picnic table, demolishing its spread, scattering hot dogs and buns. Paper napkins filled the air, to come fluttering down like king-size confetti. A gob of mustard came splattering into my left eye, catsup into my right.

Winking alternately, I beheld the longest picnic table (and the shortest picnic) ever assembled in our town. If I blinked my mustard eye, then my catsup eye, the world was an electric traffic light.

Yellow.

Red.

Yellow.

Red.

Yellow.

Red.

My gills, however, felt rather *green*.

After crashing through the canoe, we smashed to a complete stop, hitting the band. All of the band members scattered like bowling pins. I hoped this would please Sinker. His one perfect strike.

"Say," said a male voice, "I'm a member in good standing of The Knights of Saint Bingo. By golly, I could swear I've seen that contraption somewhere." He pointed at his former poker table. "Where you people from?"

"Samoa," said Sinker, as we untangled.

"That's right," said Soup, indicating our tattered ensign atop a fractured beanpole. "Here's our flag."

"We," I said, "are pearl divers."

Miss Boland appeared, brandishing her ever ready first-aid kit. "You boys look taller than usual. How come?"

Glancing down, I realized that I was standing on Janice Riker's face, while Soup stood on Eddy's. Sinker, on the other hand, was coughing up water. Clearing his throat, he said to his microphone: "Folks, this is Sinker O. Sailor, signing off and shipping out, eager to eat another mouth*water*ing bowl of Soggymushies."

As he clicked off his microphone, Sinker appeared to be both soggy and mushy. He looked sad.

"Boys," he said to us, "this might have been my final radio show. For me, it'll be *so long, WGYP,* because my contract is up, and not being renewed."

People crowded around us.

They all, contrary to what Sinker had said, had a far more positive opinion.

"Best radio show I ever heard," a lady said, "and so exciting I almost swooned."

"You bet," her husband added. "Escaping those pirates, and then down Suicide Flume. It's amazing how you radio people can fake all that action, with sound effects, and make it sound so real. Like it actual happened!"

Sinker appeared about to faint.

Yet he didn't, because two gentlemen wearing suits and neckties (a rare sight in Learning, except on a

Sunday morn) came rushing to Sinker's side. Both were smiling.

"Congratulations, Sinker," one man said. "As you know, I'm the station manager at WGYP. And today's show will make radio history!"

"Right," said the other man. "My name is Fillpot Q. Mush, president of the company that makes and sells Soggymushies." He held out a hand to Sinker O. Sailor. "For my dough, your new contract is solid with us. And that also means a pay raise."

Sinker smiled.

"That's not all," said the WGYP manager. "You deserve a free vacation. On us. Here's your ticket." He handed an envelope to Sinker.

"What is it?" Sinker asked his boss.

The station manager smiled. "A boat cruise."

Sinker fainted.

Miss Boland, however, quickly revived him, and presented him with another gift, from the entire town. A goat.

"Her name is Nannette," she said. "Now, to make sure she doesn't run away, I'll just knot her rope around your wrist."

"Thanks," said Sinker. "Thank you, everybody."

"By the way," someone asked, "where are those two troublesome pirates? They deserve a good sound whaling."

Janice and Eddy ran blubbering.

Soup and I shook hands.

"Rob, old tiger," said Soup, "we did it. We actual helped Sinker O. Sailor to broadcast a real live radio show that saved his endangered career."

I agreed. "It was worth a wetting."

"You know," said my pal, "Sinker's always rescuing people on the radio. He deserved to get rescued himself."

We looked at each other and grinned.

Yet the highlights of Sinker Day were still to come. Miss Boland gathered all of us kids together (except for Eddy and Janice) and we started to sing the anthem she'd written, to honor Sinker. During the first verse, I heard a very weird noise.

BAH-AH-AH-AH-AH-AH.

"What's that?" I asked Soup.

"That," he answered, "is a mating call. It's spring!"

Soup was right. All of a sudden, people screamed, just as the ugliest prize of the day arrived on the scene. An uninvited guest.

Buttinski.

He spotted his target, the prettiest nanny goat in town. Nannette. As he approached, she bolted, yanking Sinker with her on the other end of her rope.

"No, no, Nannette!" hollered Sinker as he sailed through the air.

Everyone ran as we sang. (Or because we sang.) The firemen sounded their siren. The mayor tried to

campaign. Our band mangled John Philip Sousa. And little old Miss Gibbons recited *The Boy Stood on the Burning Deck,* as Buttinski chased Nannette, with obvious romance in mind.

"Atta boy," yelped Mr. Amos Jubert. "Go get her!" He winked at Miss Gibbons, and tried to steal a kiss, until she politely declined by whacking him with her umbrella.

Mr. Jubert sank like a bowling ball.

"Rob," said Soup, "it all worked out. Sinker's going to have two goats instead of one. And maybe a lot more."

I spotted Norma Jean Bissell.

She was coming my way! And here I was, soaking wet, my genuine paperette sailing cap a matted mess, resembling a used Kleenex. So I couldn't fathom why Norma Jean was smiling so happily.

"Oh, Rob," she was cooing, a sound that always melted me like butter on a hot pancake, "You're so . . . You're so very . . ."

"Brave?" I asked hopefully.

She shook her head. Then whispered, "You're so *clean.*"

"I washed," I told her. "Just for you."

"I'm going to be sick," said Soup.

He left.

Bit by boisterous bit, all activity came docking to a stop. Except for the two goats, who were now chasing Eddy Tacker and Janice Riker, and butting their bottoms. Sinker had gotten free when Nannette's rope snapped.

Best of all, I was sort of alone with the opal of my ocean, Norma Jean Bissell. With heartfelt longing, I looked at her, through the catsup and mustard in my lovelorn eyes.

It was May.

17

The picnic ended. The band disbanded.

The people limped (or crawled) away, leaving one of the most unusual celebrations Learning had ever endured.

Sinker O. Sailor shook hands with Soup and me.

"Luther and Robert," he said, with a hand on my shoulder, the other on Soup's, "thank you both for understanding. For your respect. And for becoming my best friends in Learning. I'm glad I returned."

"You're our hero, sir," said Soup. "And count on Rob and me to keep all of your secrets. Just as you're keeping your job."

"Sir," I said, "you rescued us from Janice and Eddy

and helped us get our caps back. You really are a captain of courage."

"Sometime," said Soup, "perhaps Rob and I can locate your bowling ball, bring it up, and then deliver it to you."

Sinker held up a protesting hand. "No," he said. "If I take up bowling again, it'll be using a ball with holes. So let's allow our Black Pearl to rest in peace, in Wet Lake, where it somehow is destined to retire."

Sinker left in the big WGYP truck.

Soup and I watched our hero go.

We stayed behind to help Miss Boland tidy up the picnic grounds. And to tell her what a smashing success Sinker Day was. We also thanked her. Even for the anthem.

"Thank you, boys," said Miss Boland, stooping to extract a gob of relish from my ear. "Next time, you rascals won't have to handle any escort detail. I'm assigning the two of you to permanent shore duty."

We laughed. So did she.

Miss Boland departed.

"Well," I said to Soup, as we picked up the last errant paper napkin and a mustard paddle, "we're all through."

"Not quite," Soup told me.

"What's left to do?"

Soup answered by glancing at what little remained of the *Star Of Samoa*. There she lay, on land, busted and forgotten. Her mast was cracked like a broken dream.

"This is no proper grave for a great lady," Soup said. "If we leave her here, she'll be carted back to The Dump. While you were romancing Norma Jean Bissell, I noticed that her two water tanks had washed to shore. So did her seesaw."

"So what'll we do, Soup?"

"Rob, what say we sort of rig her back together? She deserves it. Then we'll flood her tanks, and scuttle her. With honor."

I nodded. "Sink her to her rest."

We did it. Reassembled, the *Star Of Samoa* slowly sank in the crick, bubbles and all. Buried at sea. Soup and I stood proudly at attention in our sailor caps at the water's edge and saluted her.

I couldn't speak. Only swallow.

"She was our first ship, Rob," said Soup. "I'm happy we gave her a decent farewell. We'll keep her ensign."

"Forever," I said, holding her flag to my heart.

Ahoy.

Robert Newton Peck has sixty books to his credit, including his highly acclaimed first novel, *A Day No Pigs Would Die,* and the sequel, *A Part of the Sky. Soup Ahoy* is the thirteenth in a series that includes *Soup* and *Soup and Me,* books all deeply rooted in rural Vermont, where Peck grew up.

He now lives in Longwood, Florida.